SAIGON WRITERS CLUB

SAIGON WRITERS CLUB

*A Distinguished Club
for Writers Who Write*

Dry Season 2022

Preface

More than 15 years ago, I acted on a crazy idea.

The idea was to organize and host a marathon race on top of a mountain range in Southwest Montana in the USA. The runners would have to run a full or half marathon (42K or 21K) on a gravel road on top of a mountain range near Yellowstone National Park. The road had an average elevation of around 2,750 meters (9,000 feet) above sea level.

I had never organized a 100-meter race before much less a full marathon of 42K. I had never even run a race of more than 5K. I definitely never tried to run any distance at an elevation of 2,750 meters. I had no idea what I was doing, but I was going to do it anyway and I hoped that enough runners would sign up to make it worthwhile. In that first year of 2008, there was a grand total of 33 runners (six full, 19 half, and eight relay runners). The next year, the race almost doubled to 52 runners (six full, 34 half, and 12 relay runners) and the year after that it almost doubled again to 92 runners (27 full, 47 half, eight relay runners, and 10 DNS [did not show up] runners).

Then something happened after that third year. The race caught the attention of marathon runners from around the USA and a handful of foreign countries. It became a national and international Bucket List destination sporting event, and for the next four years it sold out a month before race day.

This past summer (July 2022) this original marathon race, called the Madison Marathon, celebrated its 15th year of operation. The Madison Marathon is now just one of eight races of a high-altitude mountain race series called the Greater Yellowstone Adventure Series. The series races are all located near Yellowstone National Park in the high mountains of Southwest Montana and they are managed by yours truly.

What's the moral of this marathon story?

I'm still working on a good morality tale, but it seems that valid reasons eventually appear when you say WTF and just give a crazy idea a try. Need more proof?

In your hands is the **Dry Season 2022** Short Story Anthology, the result of a crazy idea called the **Saigon Writers Club**. This is the Club's second anthology. I can't say whether or not there will be a 15th anthology, but I do know there will be a third (**Rainy Season 2022**) because the Club's fourth creative writing class has already begun and the fifth and sixth classes are in planning for later this year. The short stories from these classes will be published in the third anthology. Going forward, I intend to teach as many writing classes as possible each year and to publish two short story anthologies per year for as long as there are dry seasons and rainy seasons in Vietnam.

But, it's really not up to me. Just like in the world of organized running events, athletes and wannabe athletes need to sign up and toe the starting line of a marathon. They need to commit, train, start running, and not stop running until they reach the finish line. Whatever their reason for deciding to run a marathon, they need to see that reason through to the end. They need to finish what they started.

Writers and wannabe writers are the same. It's easy to start writing a story. A key reason for launching the **Saigon Writers Club** was a firm belief that everyone in the world has a story inside of them and they want to tell their story to the world. They want their story to come out, but they often need help figuring out how to write down and tell their story. That's where I come in as a writing teacher/coach. That's what the **Saigon Writers Club's** creative writing classes are all about. With a bit of help, it's easy to start writing your own short story. It is not too easy to finish it, but I pledge to do everything I can to make that happen.

The published writers in this anthology reached their finish lines. They are from five separate countries. The settings of their stories are equally diverse. There are stories that begin more than 100 years ago to 50 years ago to today and in locations as diverse as the Netherlands, Malaysia, America, and contemporary and historical Vietnam. This is a rich collection of short stories and it was an honor to work with these writers during their creative process.

Writers write. That's what these **Saigon Writers Club** members did over the past few months. I hope you enjoy their stories as much as I did in witnessing their creation.

Thank you for the supporting the artistic community of Vietnam.

Sam Korsmoe
Founder & Teacher of the **Saigon Writers Club**
August 2022

Table of Contents

CHAPTER 1

Rivers of Destiny

By

Richard Burrage

Trần Đề, Sông Mekong (River) 1905

Death was near. Jim was strewn across the foredeck, ghostly white, ram shackled and frail. His skin was reminiscent of a frayed goose with stark red burns. His breathing was a tortured rasp, the air sounded as it was being forcibly sucked out of his lungs. Phương's father had seen him from afar entangled in the mud flats on the coast near Vĩnh Châu. He assumed that a fellow fisherman had been lost overboard. He had anchored his boat and traversed the mud flats on foot to where the tide had dumped the body.

Phương's father had never set eyes upon such a tall man, so pale and near death. His first thought had been to turn away and pray to unsee all that was before him. But he feared that the sea gods would fail to protect him in the future, allowing the storm gods to devour him in retribution. Fate had cast its shadow and his own inquisitiveness had demanded a price to be paid. Resigned, he used his nets to slowly haul Jim back to his boat, for Jim had lost all his strength.

Phương was later embarrassed that her first thought on seeing Jim was not to rush to his aid. She simply could not imagine why any man would need such a long nose? What use did it serve? Its otherworldly prominence was enhanced by the throbbing sun blisters adorning it in bright purple glory. "Purple!", the colour of death, she had yelled "Vi help" for her sister was five years wiser and would surely know what to do.

Together they washed and cleaned Jim's body and diligently placed herbs from the forest on his deep abrasions and raw blisters. After his nose, two further oddities struck Phương and Vi. The first set them both off in hysterical giggles and earnt them a slap from their mother, whom herself blushed. Phương and Vi had only seen the village boys naked. They were both more than a little shocked to learn of what grew in manhood.

The second oddity caused such a stir that the village elders came to give their opinions. A series of red lashes lay across Jim's back. They were older and healed, but too symmetrical to be an act of nature. The village elders concluded that this man must have been a slave, perhaps his escape had nearly ended his days.

For three weeks, Jim lay immobile in the wooden shack Phương called home. Gently tilting his head up five times a day, Vi and Phương would take turns to force-feed him a gruel of rice and fish broth. His soul was clearly tortured as his murmurs and cries often awoke their family long before dawn. Much to the bemusement of their mother, both Vi and Phương vied to look after Jim. They nursed this strange man who had yet to mutter a single word, as if they were jealous of who helped him more.

By week four, Jim was able to walk and wash in the river. Jim had no comprehension of where in the world he was. Perhaps this was the great land of the Manchu some now called China? Or had the sea's currents taken him back to the Dutch East Indies and the Spice Islands in the Indonesian archipelago? He knew not.

By week five Jim was lightly swimming under the watchful eyes of Vi and Phương. Jim used these moments of near solitude to unravel his fate and try to comprehend just how he had survived. What of the ship's carpenter to whom he was apprenticed? What of the Dutch sailors who had teased and tricked him endlessly? These men had taught him how to survive aboard a clipper. He spared little thought for the captain who too often had singled him out, the lone Englishman, for a dozen lashes for each of his slightest misdemeanors.

The clipper ship had been bearing northwest, back from the Spice Islands, fully loaded with nutmeg, cinnamon, pepper, chillies and stranger spices still. The clipper had been desperately trying to outrun the black clouds on the horizon and the storm which they foretold. With each league, the storm had been bearing down on them and there was neither land nor shelter in sight. All of sudden the sea had calmed accompanied by an eerie silence that preempted a wrath of destruction beyond even the most seasoned sailor's imagination.

The raging wind not only whipped the sails. It completely ripped the mast from its hold in the deck, sails begone and harpooned the mast right through the quarter deck and into the abyss. Hanging on for dear life, all Jim could see was a wall of water that stretched to the heavens. Over the howling wind, he had heard the screams of his shipmates as if they were seagulls passing overhead. The only constant for Jim had been the thump of his own heart pounding in abject fear.

Many days later, Jim had briefly stirred to see Phương's father tugging him from the depths of hell and hauling him aboard a small fishing boat. The next time Jim had awoken, it was to a beautiful maiden. Perhaps she was a sea nymph that fellow sailors had spoken of in whispers?

Yet this maiden, Phương, bore a wooden spoon with a life-giving salty fish broth.

During a dawn swim whilst his chaperones watched from the overhang, Jim was joined by the village boys who whooped, splashed and laughed with him. Jim's spirits were lifted. He looked to the sky and gave thanks to his Gods for this generous family. They had saved him from being devoured by whatever lay in the depths of the sea. He was wholly aware that this family had barely enough to feed themselves. He endeavoured to be timid with his appetite. He resolved to bring food to this family's table and to stop being a burden.

Jim needed to learn their sing-song tongue, to flourish and to prove himself. He knew this was the only way he would ever find his way home to London and her docks, a quart of ale and his mother. He had not embraced her since his ill-fated departure aboard the Dutch clipper from London's docks on a chilling February dawn in 1904. Most certainly he had to square up to his father and admonish him for all the woes he had suffered at his whimsical antics. His father had placed Jim, his only son, in servitude to help settle his own debts.

Phương's father was torn by what to do about Jim. Whilst affable, he was yet another mouth to feed and was rapidly depleting their rice stores. It played on his mind and he bemoaned his fate and deliberated his choices at length with the village elders.

Trần Đề, Sông Mekong (River)1905

Jim spent his mornings working with wood, making moorings to secure boats, pens for pigs and small enclosures to offer privacy for the villagers' morning constitution. The villagers had chuckled to learn that they could relieve themselves from on high, using his raised lavvy on a jetty which was just five hundred steps downriver. Jim's biggest structure made him the darling of the village. He built a raised wooden jetty that stretched from the banks into the deepest channel in the river. For the villagers, this was a gift from the heavens. They no longer had to trudge through mud flats when the tide was low to unload their bounty. Phương shone with pride.

Phương and Vi spent the late afternoons teaching Jim Vietnamese on long, slow walks. There were so many new words that Jim's tongue could not keep pace with his thoughts. Both Phương and Vi were very amused by his attempts. The sound of their laughter became a constant hymn in the village. Phương was just eighteen years old, but for every word Jim mastered, Phương learned four in English. Vi had shown little interest in learning Jim's tongue, but she loved to tease them both for their garbled attempts.

The village elders agreed that Jim's prowess with woodwork was greatly benefiting their village. They resigned to contribute to his up-keep collectively and much to the dismay of Phương's father suggested that Vi become his wife. After all, Vi remained unmarried at the grand old age of 23 years!

On hearing this news from the village leader's eldest daughter, who was the source of all gossip, Vi retreated back to her chores, net making and fish drying. She was rarely to be seen accompanying Phương and Jim on their sunset walks, for she held absolutely no interest in marrying such a strange long-nosed man and was woe to entice any village gossip.

Phương was grateful to spend more time alone with Jim. His bright eyes shone with constant wonder and his energy and laughter were infectious. Phương often lay awake at night wondering what it would be like to lie with a man, this particular man. She would turn from her sister, who slept alongside her and bite her bottom lip when she felt herself moisten in response to her secret thoughts.

Trần Đề, Sông Mekong (River)1906

On the first day of spring for the village feast, Phương unwrapped her only áo dài, which had not been worn in many months. The long white pants, overlaid by a long straight shimmering red dress, fell almost to her ankles and extenuated her height. She was already a head taller than all the other women in the village and many of the men. This was the first time Jim had witnessed her adorned in colour. Jim's reaction was just as she had hoped. Her elegance and beauty took his breath away. The dress held her perfect posture and made her appear both regal and elegant. Jim's daydreams were fraught with possibilities.

Three days of celebrations followed. There was an abundance of sticky rice, broiled pork, fried fish and a constant stream of dishes blending a delicious sweetness finely honed against an undercurrent of sourness. It was all washed down by lashings of coarse rice wine that would make any sailor's head spin.

Sitting by the bank at sunset, Phương felt an unabashed touch on her arm whilst exchanging words for all that they could see along the river bank. Laughing, Jim had lightly touched her forearm causing him a strange sensation. He realised that he had not touched nor been touched by another since his return to health. Phương struggled to hide her surprise and to hold her arm in place whilst trying to keep herself from blushing.

Just two nights later, Phương was startled when Jim's tongue pierced her lips and found her own. She braced herself, half wanting him to stop whilst wondering how best to respond. She had never seen, let alone experienced, such a strange affection. Coupling in her village was a hurried affair under the cover of darkness or on a secluded river bank.

There was little choice when one family shared a single reed mat to sleep upon.

It began awkwardly, but very gradually she relaxed and responded. She suddenly felt her loins burning with desire and quickly backed away, frightened by her own body and lightheadedness. Slowly they embraced again and Jim held her tight and ever so slowly she explored Jim's face and neck. Jim had barely more romantic experience than Phương, only having ever kissed one woman passionately in his 23 years. It felt as if Phương was inhaling him, a snuggle, not a kiss. Whilst strange, the affection was endearing and Jim yearned for more.

Phương made it very clear to Jim that their affections must remain secret. She would reach for his hand only when the village children had retreated and they were far away from prying eyes. Jim's heart was heavy with foreboding, for he did not wish to repay this family with disrespect or shame. But he was smitten with Phương and relished her touch and affections. Their feelings were mutual.

It was many weeks before the rains came and their desires overcame their sensibilities. Phương's sharp pain was quickly followed by a head-spinning explosion of joy within the depths of her lotus flower. The heavens opened and she embraced his lust with enthusiasm. She had recalled her own giggles at seeing his manhood when she first washed his frail body many months before. How on earth his manhood and her lotus flower could join together left her in wonder. Slowly they learned together, that which the other enjoyed. Their over-eager early encounters moved from a hurried almost animalistic lust towards a more relaxed and euphoric love-making.

Their mutual joy carried them through the long rainy season as the river rose to new heights, flooding the plains around with a deep velvet blanket of rich silt. The floods nourished the surrounding rice fields and settled into low-lying still lakes. Lakes that stretched to the limits of the horizon. Jim could not imagine the source of so much water. The river now caressed the surface of Jim's raised jetty, which only four months previously had stretched 30 steps to where the channel was deep enough for the fishing boats. Jim was in awe at the power of this great river that made London's Thames River look like a quaint stream.

Eventually, the rains ceased and the mud baked and cracked into deep chasms. Gradually the river retreated. Jim's raised jetty became more useful by the day. The cicadas fell silent, the humidity rose and the heat stifled all it touched. However, more oppressing was the deep despair Phương felt for the inexcusable consequences of her actions. The shame on her family would be irreproachable and that she must turn away from Jim was inexplicable.

Phương did not know whether she cried more in self-pity or for the hurt she was clearly causing Jim. Fate had struck, but Phương made a choice to change both their destinies. She could not hold Jim back in her village forever. To stay together would have seen them repeating the lives of her parents. Long ago on the banks of the Mekong, anxiously awaiting the safe return of her father after a great storm, she had made a wager. A wager with the heavens and all their gods that she would alter the fate passed on by her ancestors. Her own destiny was to be released from the whims of the storm and sea gods at any price. She would not grow old in a fishing village called Trần Đề, on the Mekong River!

She spurned Jim without warning, without explanation and left him rudderless in an ocean of heartache. His father always said that he never understood the mind of a woman and Jim finally grasped his meaning. No rhyme or reason was forthcoming. He could hardly find a moment alone with her. He withdrew and would disappear for days at a time, wandering further upriver seeking solace through distraction.

One evening Jim learned that his neighbour was traveling the follow-ing day to a pottery village a day's walk north of Sài Gòn. During his time at sea, Jim had heard many a tale of the great ports of the Orient such as Melaka, Penang, Sài Gòn, Canton and Ningbo. Sài Gòn was described as the Pearl of the Orient. Why not go along? He needed to start afresh, to find a new adventure and perhaps, just perhaps, find a berth for his long journey back home to the docks of London and a quart of ale.

He said a long heartfelt goodbye to Vi, her mother and her father. He ate with the village elders. He searched the village and the nearby river banks for Phương, but alas could not find her. It was clear that she was hiding and would not bid him farewell. Before daybreak, he was on his way.

Sài Gòn 1906

By bringing Minh Anh fatherless into the world, Phương had made a choice to leave Trần Đề, her home village on the most westerly estuary of the formidable Nine Dragons River as the Mekong River is colloquially called. To stay would have brought nothing but misfortune to her family. The village elders had made that abundantly clear.

Already two months pregnant, Phương had slowly weaved her way by bicycle, ferry and sheer determination the 200 kilometers to Sài Gòn. The acclaimed Pearl of the Orient harboured the largest contingent of foreigners in the Orient. Ironically, the fate that had brought Jim to their shores had also treated Phương to a heavenly sent linguistic gift. She had been a far more pliable and culpable student than Jim. Her English was superb while Jim's Vietnamese was pigeon at best and his best normally required a few cups of rice wine to surface.

After a few months of scavenging around the Phú Hòa market and doing odd jobs, she had given birth to her handsome boy, upon whom she doted, much as her father had doted on her. With two mouths to feed, she had deliberately and earnestly finessed her way into the household of Ping Loh, Sài Gòn's wealthiest merchant and trader. Being accepted into Ping's household as a maid was the culmination of weeks of diligently watching, following and befriending his household staff. Her way in was greased with promissory bribes, a proportion of the coin earnt for her first year. She had to wear borrowed clothes for her final presentation before Ping.

Ping hailed from Macau. With his family's trading history, Ping had tied up much of the trade with the Chinese in the North and the Indonesian tribes in the Spice Islands in the far South. Ping's father was a Portuguese trader and his mother hailed from Canton. Legend had it, that she was a former courtesan to a court mandarin for the Qing emperor.

Like all the other Việts in Sài Gòn, Phương knew Ping by reputation only. His great wealth and trading acumen was embodied in his palatial home. Ping's mansion, subtly decorated with opium poppies, overlooked the Sài Gòn River and the Thủ Thiêm parish church across the water. Ping's mansion stood three levels tall above the shacks and go-downs of the area and is a mere five-minute walk from the docks at Dragon Wharf and the equally daunting Custom's House. Made of tall symmetrical stones, the likes of which Phương had never seen before and the mansion reeked of power and strength. Visitors would steel themselves before entering, intimidated, as if a mysterious force may sap them of all their energy.

Within six months of joining Ping's household, Phương mustered enough pigeon Cantonese to bargain with the merciless Canton hags who controlled the food stalls in the newly built market just southwest of the docks. Her Cantonese, though limited, was already adept at the foulest of insults. She could use words that she would never dream of saying in her native Vietnamese. Phương enjoyed her market errands.

In the mansion, she was warned to never speak until spoken to and she was rarely spoken to.

Ping had never shown any interest in Phương nor for that matter any of his household staff. He was cordial only with his office clerks, but they too feared his wrath.

It was a slip of the tongue, combined with the power of poor calligraphy, that changed Phương's prospects. This put her on a trajectory that she had never dared dream of. On this auspicious day, a sour-faced Russian merchant, the broadest man Phương had ever seen, was waiting for his appointment in Ping's garden. As she served him iced tea, Phương felt sorry for him. Given his huge bearing, she felt that his appetite could surely match the whole of her village. She pitied the tailor who had to fashion this Sour Face's breeches.

Sour Face and his secretary were speaking in a mix of English and a strange tongue which she assumed to be Russian. It heralded a harshness, the abrupt tones sounded as if the secretary was being scolded. It was clear to Phương that her English was far superior to theirs. The secretary was seeking affirmation that six-gold tales was the correct asking price and four gold tales was the lowest price that they could entertain.

Three hours later and with Phương serving yet more tea to Ping, the negotiations between Ping and the two Russians were still ongoing. They were assisted by the Padre, the only accomplished linguist in Sài Gòn. The Padre was an animated socialite who was as comfortable tending to his Catholic flock as he was sharing stories with the rickshaw drivers. Ping loathed relying on him as little occurred in Sài Gòn that the Padre did not know.

The Padre was explaining in Cantonese to Ping that if the Russians agreed to his price of five gold tales they would then expect Ping to pay the Customs House given his cordial relationships in Sài Gòn. Thus, their business was coming to a close.

Phương, who had been listening intently, decided to seize this opportunity to help her paymaster. But how to do so? Ping was barely aware of her existence. She coughed as if to speak, but panic struck and she felt the blood rise to her cheeks as she swiftly turned away. What followed happened in a trance for Phương, she felt as if she had left her body and was watching herself from a great height. If this went awry, she would be back working around the market by dawn in order to feed her son Minh Anh.

She slowly and carefully placed her tray on the edge of Ping's desk, grasped his quill and gingerly scribed 肥胖的妓女, 值四兩金 on a piece of paper. Not knowing how to write in formal Cantonese nor the character for Russian nor merchant, she scribbled what she could, which read: "Fat mother of a whore, bottom price four tales." She then tried to compose herself, turned to Ping and signaled to the desk with her eyes before dashing out of the room in a quiver of nerves.

Ping was aghast. Not even his private secretary would dare use his quill. This maid had the audacity to do so and then gaze directly at him. Ping was rarely left speechless and if not for the refined company present, he would have struck her for such impertinence.

As his guests sipped their tea, he meandered over to his desk and took a double-take. On his second reading, he uncyphered the poor Cantonese and smiled inwardly. Affably, he turned back to his adversaries, one tale richer. One gold tale was more than Phương would earn in a lifetime.

Ping knew that the advantage to be gleaned from a gifted linguist was even greater than loose tongues. His network of connections and paid spies from Macau, Canton, along the great Ch'ang Chiang River and in Sài Gòn coupled with his own ability to speak both Portuguese and Cantonese had kept his trading fortunes thriving.

As he studied Phương who stood twitching nervously before him with her eyes demurely lowered, he realised that fate was handing him a prized jewel. Ping did not find her beautiful but she was strangely tall and graceful for a Việt. That she spoke the English tongue was her true worth and her pigeon Cantonese confirmed to him that she was innately gifted.

She was a lotus seed to nourish and grow into a blossoming flower. A flower that with his light touch may well help him open more trade with the ignorant Europeans who could not speak his father's native Portuguese. It was thus decided that Phương would cease her maid duties immediately. She would study Cantonese each morning in the gardens with an assigned scholar and work alongside his private secretary in his suite of offices each afternoon. Destiny had entangled their fortunes and was keeping fate at bay.

Sài Gòn 1912

Destiny or fate? Which will prevail? Phương must apologise and face the consequences. She must ensure that destiny prevails over all that fate has thrown in her path. Destiny, Phương knows all too well, is a choice. Timing plays an oversized role in destiny. That and the presence of mind to recognise that a choice is indeed available.

Phương must explain. She owes it to her father. She owes it to her son Minh Anh who turns six years at Tết, the onset of spring. Most of all, she owes it to Jim. Her actions had set him on his journey, no doubt one that he thought was his rightful destiny. Yet unbeknown to Jim, she had pushed his fate aft and to this day continued to intercede from afar to alter his destiny.

Fate, on the other hand, is like the gale-force wind that often hammered down on the foresails of her father's fishing boat and prevented him from hauling in his nets and returning home safely. On many occasions, Phương had foolishly ventured out into a typhoon, stumbling frantically towards the estuary of the Mekong River. Threading her way down bracken banks and through the mangrove roots as far as her scrapped legs would carry her. All the while, desperately searching the horizon for the turquoise ribbon she had tied onto the pinnacle of the foresail. Her nightmares reinforced in her a constant fear of her father's demise at the hands of the storm gods.

In the last great storm, in the Year of the Dragon when she was just 15 years old, Phương was convinced the storm gods had taken her father when he had not returned by daybreak. She had shaken uncontrollably and lost the will to all but breathe. For two days straight, she sat like an immovable rock, oblivious of the mosquitoes feasting on her and stared out from the estuary. Just as dusk descended on the third day, she glimpsed the turquoise ribbon atop of the floundering mast. As her heart rose, she wagered with the heavens and all their gods that she would alter the fate passed onto her by her ancestors. Her own destiny was to be released from the whims of the storm and sea gods. At any price.

Fate is the woes of our ancestors, the will of the gods and their ill omens, unfortunate timing and most of all our own egos and the egos of those upon whom we chance. Fate, egos and the staggering ignorance that inevitably ensues make for a formidable adversary against destiny.

———————

Sài Gòn 1912

Today was the day. Phương had set the wheels in motion to conjure up a little serendipity. This day would be the beginning. Today would allow destiny to prevail, despite what fate may throw in Phương's path. The unravelling of the past six years, to apologise, to explain and to face the consequences of her choices.

Serendipity was how she desired Jim to view their chance meeting at the Customs House. As she applied some light powder to her face, she pondered whether her interference in Jim's business dealings should be made known to him or kept forever obscured. She was all too conscious that a man's ego could be too readily bruised.

Jim's shipment of tea from upcountry would leave the dock this morning and her spies had told her that he would be meeting the Chief of Customs that morning to bargain for lower taxes. She and Ping would coincidentally be there to pay their own duties on inbound shipments.

On first seeing Jim, her heart froze momentarily and with a small gasp, she threw him a warning shot with her eyes. Twenty-four years of family values countenanced a gravitational force that prevented her from embracing him with joyful and raucous laughter. Phương knew it was unwise to reveal her shared history with this long-nosed Englishman, especially to her paymaster Ping. She could not let Ping connect any of her circumspect actions which had too often been veiled support to Jim from afar.

"Ping," said the overbearing Chief of Customs. "This is the Long Nose, the Englishman, the one who seems to think my men cannot count and only shows thirty percent of his goods in his loading dockets."

Following Phương's translation, he continued to address her, "Sister, you have surely met Long Nose at the docks." He was momentarily confused by her lack of acknowledgment. Phương had most certainly sought him out to persist in the release of Jim's last shipment. The Chief of Customs harboured her reaction for later consideration and continued regardless.

"Now Long Nose, this is Ping Loh who always has dockets that match his cargo and knows best how to treat a poor old Chief of Customs to his advantage. Perhaps he could teach you a thing or two. Now go and load your goods Long Nose!"

Jim was speechless. A rare event. But not for the reasons that both Ping and the Chief of Customs assumed. His heart was racing and he was perspiring as if he were lifting a mast single-handedly. He merely nodded in polite deference and retreated in shock.

Phương! Was it really his first love? Was it love or had that been youthful lust? There was rarely a day when she did not enter his thoughts. Why the warning shot? Why the anonymity? Why was she with the shrewd trader Ping? What on earth was she doing in Sài Gòn, let alone at the Custom's House?

Jim sat warily on the docks. His heart was still pounding, not unlike that fateful day in the great storm, the day that nearly ended his life and yet led to him being re-born, courtesy of Phương's encouragement.

Why did Phương spurn him all those years ago in Trần Đề? He had never been able to thank her. For she was the catalyst. Phương, her family, and their village had wholeheartedly nursed him back to health and later strengthened him before she had ultimately given him her unabashed love and affections. What mystified him the most was the abrupt ending even though it had spurred him on his way to Sài Gòn. Truth be told, he had needed to escape the confines of the village of Trần Đề alongside the Mekong River. But he sorely regretted never embracing Phương one last time to bid her farewell. It dawned on him that he would very much like to do so again.

Sài Gòn 1912

Phương observed Jim waiting outside the Customs House as Ping left. She held back to finalise details with the Custom clerks. Trembling with anticipation as she approached Jim, she held his gaze and falteringly stammered.

"Jim it is with great delight that I, that I, lay my eyes on you once more. I have much to tell you and will seek you out soon. Here too many eyes observe us. I will seek you out."

"Wait let's talk now," demanded Jim.

"I will find you," she responded as she abruptly turned and walked away along the river bank.

Jim hesitated before deciding to trail her. He followed at 200 steps distant, enamored with the elegance of her gliding stride and stature. He watched as she entered the gates of the finest mansion along the river, which all the traders knew, housed both the home and office suites of Ping Loh.

Jim was confused. He imagined a stream of wild scenarios that would place Phương in Ping's mansion. None of which added up and he was left with nothing but a multitude of questions.

Commandeering his own clerk's bicycle, he waited for the sight of Phương near Ping's mansion. As a throng of clerks left in the late afternoon, she emerged on a bicycle. He gingerly followed her as she pedaled her way northwest beyond the limits of downtown Sài Gòn where the foreign traders rarely traversed.

After passing through the Phú Hòa market, Phương turned into an alley just wide enough for two people. Drenched in his own sweat, Jim halted and watched from the alley's entrance. The alley was a stark contrast to the squalor of discarded offal, fish scales, coconut husks and a sea of unwanted rotting vegetables around the market.

As Phương dismounted, he heard a cry of joy as a small boy with a gleaming smile ran to her embrace. His giggles of delight were carried down the narrow alley as Phương lifted him effortlessly with a twirl into her arms. She carried him into one of the perfectly maintained wooden houses that were adorned with a rainbow of brightly coloured bougainvillea.

Jim dismounted and began to walk towards the house hoping to surprise Phương. As he approached, the boy reared out of the house with a shriek of laughter to join the other children playing in the alley. Jim paused and took a deep breath to ready himself, but was startled as he noticed that the boy was different from all the other children. He watched him play and realised that this boy must be mixed, a Eurasian perhaps, his skin was paler, his eyes rounder and his nose a little more pronounced.

Jim unconsciously recoiled. His dreams of a warm embrace and holding Phương disintegrated into hard specks of cold English hail. His heart hardened into a block of clay dried by the Mekong sun. The boy was clearly Eurasian. Ping Loh must be the father, a kept woman, a mistress perhaps? Certainly not even a second wife to be living in this alley behind the squalor of Phú Hòa market.

As the group of boys stood wide-eyed, staring at the strange white man at the end of the alley, they broke into hysteria, laughing and pointing for want of an appropriate response. Phương rounded the gate to seek out the source of so much joviality. She locked eyes with Jim, but her smile quickly waned into a grimace, for a picture tells a thousand words. Jim's face was a sheen of disgust and repugnancy.

Jim hastily turned and walked back. He was trembling uncontrollably with fury as his thoughts swam with ugly scenarios. Tears welled in Phương's eyes. She averted her face from the children as tears silently rolled down her cheeks. Her yearning to be understood, for Jim to empathise with her choices, was just too much to bear. Indoors she rolled herself into a tight coil and sobbed.

Jim's heart turned cold toward Phương. Jealousy consumed his whole being. With his ego in shatters, he manically rode back to his lodgings to stew in a sea of hatred. A hatred solely directed at Ping, the trader from Macau, whom fate had thrust in his path.

Sài Gòn 1912

Jim met Deveaux, a merchant sailor turned plantation owner in the Café de Marseille. After the obligatory British versus French ridicule, Deveaux and Jim traded sordid sailors' tales of their exploits in Batavia, Medan, Melaka, and Penang.

A few rums later, Deveaux turned a little morose, belittling the prices he was receiving this season from the shrewd Ping Loh. As the holder of the largest peppercorn crop in the province, Deveaux had come to Sài Gòn to confront Ping whose agents in the central highlands held a monopoly on both the pepper and coffee markets. They were driving prices down below a subsistence level. Deveaux had not managed to meet with Ping, having been repeatedly turned away from the gates of his mansion and was bemoaning the man's arrogance.

Other traders had warned Jim away from dealing in pepper, noting that the trade was more than controlled by Ping, it was enforced. No one was foolish enough to cross over into Ping's domain.

Jealousy drove Jim as he sought to undercut Ping Loh from his source of pepper in the hills of Đăk Lăk. A mere three-day horseback journey from the hill station of Đà Lạt, where those who could afford to do so, retreated to escape Sài Gòn's heat and humidity. Enterprising and hardened French plantation owners had enjoyed great success harvesting peppercorn, tea and coffee in those highland valleys. Ping was adept at distributing that pepper at a great profit, far and wide, through his trade networks.

Jim convinced himself that he was a believer in Adam Smith's free markets, as he made his way through the cool, green and sleepy valleys around Buôn Ma Thuột. He was nervously rationalising his own deal-making. He had bargained hard with Deveaux during his two-day visit. Deveaux was an excellent host serving copious food, wine and stories that ran until the dawn light spread across the mist-laden valleys to the east.

The two men grew to respect one another and became willing conspirators. For different reasons, neither wished for Ping's hold on the pepper trade to be single-handed. Jim extended his resources to the limit and could not stomach any mishaps. He needed to quickly sell on the pepper before his promissory notes became due.

———————————

Sài Gòn 1912

Ping Loh was livid, pacing across his suite of offices.

"He looks like a ghost, smells like cow's milk and has the blue eyes of a *Gweilo* incarnate," he shouted demanding from no one in particular to know who this young arrogant upstart was. This man with a long nose and a strange tongue.

Phương knew that Jim was putting himself in mortal danger by cutting out Ping from his main source of highland black pepper. Phương had not grasped that Jim's foolish endeavour was the result of his presumptions, ego and ignorance after seeing her with Minh Anh.

Yet again, she would need to intercede and protect Jim from fate. Unbeknown to Jim, Phương had already used her position to secretly play a guiding role in Jim's trades and recent successes. The rumours whispered in his ear by the serving girl at the tea house and the old French seaman at the riverside bar Café de Marseille had been directed by Phương. The charlatan arrested just prior to Jim advancing him a down payment was at Phương's intervention. The ready passage of Jim's goods through customs was not, as Jim believed, due to his charisma and plying of inferior gifts. Rather it was a favour handsomely paid for by Phương to the Chief of Customs.

She tried to seek Jim out and advise him on a better course of action. For three days straight, she had waited for Jim at the Salon de Thé, this was after daily hand-delivered invitations. For three days straight, he had not appeared! Phương was saddened that Jim was not at least inquisitive enough to meet. How was she to warn him of the impending danger? Men are so stubborn and even more foolish.

Ping was not idle. He connived a plan to deal with Jim, the upstart with the long nose. Ping would not dirty his own hands, but would callously orchestrate Jim's financial ruin. Others would deal with Jim when he could not pay his promissory notes.

Sài Gòn 1912

Ping's first ruse was too easy. Jim fell for it hook, line and sinker. Ping enlisted Mai, one of the many hostesses that he used to help him entertain guests in Chợ Lớn, the Chinese enclave close to Sài Gòn. That a woman's guile with a splattering of flirtations could readily reduce a hard trader to pliable clay never ceased to amaze Ping.

Mai expressed fascination with Jim's pepper, their fragrance and its origins. She bargained hard as if he held the only peppercorn left in all of the Orient. Surely any one of the French traders would have caved at her elegance and beguile. Jim had persevered and won himself a fair price and a healthy profit. To bless the deal, Mai suggested a light supper and drinks. The grog they drank was far from rum. It was made from rice, harsh but guaranteed to loosen lips and legs if Jim played his cards right. And he did. Three hours later they lay on soaked sheets, squandering in the aftermath of their love-making. Jim had finally met his match. He was not convinced that he had made love to Mai at all. She had led the whole embrace and was not shy to let all within earshot know that she was fulfilled.

Jim awoke from his slumber behind the Café de Marseille content and happy despite his starched throat and pounding head. Jim hoped he would spend many more evenings with Mai. Jim had not pondered such thoughts after laying with a woman since his first love Phương. If that had indeed been true love? Mai was clearly smart and happy to strike a bargain in a world of men. She was just damn voluptuous!

It suddenly dawned on Jim that he was alone. With lightning speed, he rolled over and with an arched back and stretched arm seized his satchel from under the cot. Trepidation overcame him, blood rose to his temples and the pain in his head sharpened. In his heart of hearts, he knew, but he did not want to believe. The bag did not feel empty. Perhaps he would smile, laugh and lay with Mai again. Alas, all the coin was gone, just like her, gone. Six weeks of hard work, gone! He knew the pepper would have been collected from the go-down and also be long gone.

Jim learned from Pascale, the barkeep, that Mai had long since left with a sweet smile and a generous tip. Jim punched right through the wooden sleave, oblivious of the blood dripping around the splinters. He threw a slew of curses at his own reflection above the crouching barkeep's head. He was furious with himself for falling into this honey trap. His penchant for grog would be the ruin of him. He blamed it on the 20 months at sea when any near escape from pirates or storms put a smile on the God-fearing captain's face as he ordered a swig of rum for all.

Jim was left to face the blinding sun of daylight with yet another unpaid bar chit, an empty stomach, a head soarer than his blooded hand and a burning desire to turn the tide.

Sài Gòn 1912

To turn the tide, Jim needed financing. He had promissory notes due and more deliveries pending. Mai's ruse could be the ruin of him. The French financers never held any interest in supporting Jim's endeavours. They saw him as a flag, a proxy, for the British who had already cornered trade with Burma, Malaya and China. The French humoured him, but there was little love lost.

Jim had no choice but to approach the devious money lenders in Chợ Lớn where the outrageous interest rates were calculated daily. Jim had a history there, so he was greeted with a wide yet greedy smile. He had seen the missing hands of those who had not met repayments promptly. He had heard stories of those who had been carved up and left on their doorsteps. A stark reminder to all that tried to cross their notorious triad enforcers.

The money lenders were given the nod of assent from Ping within hours of Jim's approach. He wanted Jim laden with debt. The day after Jim had paid his promissory notes for pending pepper deliveries, Deveraux awoke to a mutiny amongst his pepper pickers.

The uprising was ostensibly organised by the anti-colonial, nationalist movement that hitherto had only been seen further north in Quảng Nam. These earlier uprisings were a stain on French colonialism, which saw the mass execution of too many and the imprisoning of other patriots on the island prison of Poulo Condore. Deveraux found himself caught in a political arena beyond his control as the French provincial administrators sought to intercede.

Far too quickly, Jim found himself in a triage from hell. In debt to the triads, no goods could be delivered and no trades could be made. The debt collectors would come calling, for unbeknown to Jim, they would soon be dutifully informed of his woes by Ping.

––––––––––

Sài Gòn 1912

Phương found Jim sitting on the terrace at the Grand Hôtel De La Rotonde. With his head in his hands, captivated by the slowly dripping coffee from the silver filter atop his glass and onto the sweet condensed milk. Jim imagined his blood, ever so slowly draining away to splatter onto a white sea of despair.

Phương sat unnoticed and watched in silence before laying her hand softly atop of Jim's. Only at this point did Jim emerge from his reverie and become aware of Phương's guiding hand. Phương was distraught at the shell of a man he had so quickly become. His face was drawn, his once sparkling eyes dulled and he was fighting back tears of shame.

"Jim, what you done? Why you cross Ping?" she implored. "You know how powerful he?"

"It is not Ping," retorted Jim. His angst towards Phương forgotten. "There is an uprising and my goods cannot be delivered. I owe the money lenders and I have nothing left to trade. I am ruined, I will have to run or I may lose my life."

"There no uprising. The patriot Phan Chu Trinh and his gang are behind bars on Con Dao Island. It is Ping. The money lenders....also Ping," said Phương. "Even Mai, oh yessy mister, I heard about Mai, an agent of Ping! Any peppercorn Deveraux try send to Sài Gòn will never leave the highlands. You crossed Ping and he will ruin you. You must be smarter!"

"Ping?" says Jim dumbfounded and stuttering. "But he is your lover and keeper, are you not an agent of Ping?"

"Oh my God, you big fool Jim," screamed Phương. "He is my employer and no more! I am his translator in trade making with my Việt brothers and sisters and also with those who speak the English tongue that you taught me so good."

"But, but I saw your child," stammered Jim.

"But! But, but, no more Jim! Now listen," chastised Phương.

"When this market has one strong seller, you ply your goods in another market. You are in Ping's world here. Get word to Deveraux to send whatever pepper he has to the port of Hội An, south of the imperial city of Hue. Do so quickly and keep secret, very secret. You, you Jim, you take a berth to Hội An straight away."

"To where?" stammered Jim.

"Hội An, the port three days north up the coast. Seek out An Trần. He is Hokkien Chinese, he has big hate for Ping. He was ousted from Sài Gòn port by Ping, three years back. But now he makes a big, very big, junk trade to the port of Nagasaki in the Japans. Explain your plight, he will buy your pepper, if only to be a mosquito on Ping's neck. Perhaps you ask he give you credit Jim, to buy more?" said Phương continuing.

"Now please listen me, take me advice, go and go now, bad people are searching for you. When you return and have paid money lenders, we talk, I have much to tell. I have much to say and I big hope you stop and listen me! Now I must go, I not be seen with you."

With that Phương disappeared down the boulevard. Jim baffled by a jumble of thoughts, drank down the sweetened rich brown café in one shot and went quickly on his way.

As Jim rounded a corner, he shivered as if he were being plunged into an ice-cold sea. His intuition sensed the danger too late. He fell to his knees as a large wooden stave took his legs out from beneath him, closely followed by a barrage of feet. Too many feet kicked at his ribs and his face. He rolled into a defensive position protecting his head as if being attacked by a wild animal. The battering rained down on his thighs, ribs and back. His breathing was laboured and he felt his consciousness slipping away in a dizzying cocktail of pain and panic. Fate had found him and the triads held his life on a precipice.

The kicks abruptly halted. His head was yanked up by a golden lock of his hair. "Three days... long nose, three days and we collect money. No money and we slice you open like jack fruit, piece by piece," he heard.

Then they were gone. Jim lay on his back gasping for breath, watching as if in a dream, a solitary cloud drift across a pale sky devoid of colour from the sheer brightness. Oh, the wonder of life. Oh, to live pondered Jim, the eternal optimist.

Gathered around him debating his fate was a gaggle of women who plied their wares in the main boulevards of downtown Sài Gòn. From cigarillos, Le Courrier Saigonnais, café, noodles, fried cakes to trinkets, they had it all. They surfaced to tend to Jim as soon as the triads departed. Their cries down the boulevard drew the city guard. A motley pair of poorly paid former farmers who were tasked with clearing the main thorough fairs of drunks, prostitutes, the dissolute and pilfering street urchins. Their patch only extended from the port to the Padre's church. Beyond these city limits, it really was each man and woman for themselves.

Jim was humiliated by their lack of concern and abrupt dismissal. They merely laughed and look anywhere but at him. Jim knew that this reaction was the only way that they could cope with his self-inflicted loss of face. As his blood pressure rose, he staggered away in disgust and accidentally bumped into an unsuspecting Padre who stumbled to the ground. The Padre had been determinedly seeking out the city guard in the hope that they may help him remove some slumbering drunken French sailors from his pulpit.

The gaggle of women, whilst trying to hide their own embarrassed laughter, pulled out low-lying stools for Jim and the Padre to sit on. They kindly passed them tea. Jim and the Padre took in their own circumstance and spontaneously broke into chuckles at the foolish sight that they had become. Jim seized awkwardly from a shaft of pain that shot up from his ribs. The Padre took in Jim's cuts and bruises, settled in and extended an ear of friendship. The Padre was well aware of Jim's predicament but he politely listened as Jim shared his recent woes.

The Padre retorted with a little straight-talking wisdom; "You have a longer nose than a Breton! But unfortunately, not the sight to see what lies directly in front of you. Who do you think is paying for the city guard's lunch Long Nez? To that matter who do you think pays for mine? Everything you see about us is kept safe and in order by Ping Loh! Why would you make such a powerful foe Long Nez?"

The Padre was on a roll and continued on mercilessly "And as for this Phương, she is not his lover you fool! But, Mon Dieu, she is both beautiful and brilliant. She speaks his tongue and yours, Englishman. She helps him in his trade and is better informed than his private secretary on the latest spice prices and shipments in and out of this port. You could do far worse than to heed her advice Long Nez."

Sài Gòn 1912

As dusk vanished the day, Jim sat near the river gangway to wait and pondered his fate. The speed at which darkness enveloped him was matched only by the sudden onslaught of chatter from the cicadas and toads competing to fill the void.

He had nowhere to run, nowhere to hide and no resources to fight back against Ping nor the money lenders and their triad enforcers. His ill-placed jealously had turned fate against him. Phương had interceded to turn the tide and perhaps, just perhaps, turn disaster into an opportunity. The tide was turning and his boat to Hội An would depart with it.

Phương, concealed by the night, was already onboard the Hội An bound ship, watching Jim from astern. She silently prayed that he would heed her advice and board. She knew that he was now racing against time, to make good on his promissory notes before fate cornered him. Her heartbeat skipped a beat as his stride reached the gangway and he walked onto the ship. Destiny trumped fate, this time.

Phương was melancholic as she watched Sài Gòn grow smaller and dimmer as the ship headed down the Sài Gòn River to join the Mekong River. From there, the storm gods willing, they would reach the estuary and hug the coastline for a three-day journey to Hội An. The boat would bypass her fishing village Trần Đề, which sits near the most westerly of the Nine Dragon's estuaries. Six years earlier, this was where she had first laid eyes on Jim strewn across the foredeck of her father's fishing boat.

Oh, how she would love to have returned to the bosom of her family and the butterflies of joy that rose within her every time that she remembered her early encounters with Jim. The strange reedy, blistered and long-nosed man teetering at death's door whom her father had brought home. The man who was entwined with her own destiny and that of their son, Minh Anh.

As Phương threaded her way to the foredeck and towards the embrace of her one true love, she knew that despite all she had done to guide Jim, she had yet to right her own wrongs. She had yet to declare her true love and wipe Jim's fate clear away. Fate has an insatiable appetite; it is always ready to resurface and deal an unjust hand. The death sentence was now averted. Her love sake's fate had been re-written yet again. Destiny, albeit at her guile, had triumphed.........for now.

The End

Richard Burrage

Richard Burrage is an Englishman living in Sài Gòn, Vietnam with his three daughters. He has lived in Sài Gòn for the past 25 years. By day he advises the businesses he founded long ago in both Vietnam and Indonesia.

Richard left London, England for Bombay, India in 1992 and since then has spent far too much time travelling and observing diverse cultures stretching from Japan to Cambodia.

Rivers of Destiny is the premise for an unwritten saga, an adventurous tale with more delights and hardships. Rivers of Destiny traces Richard's experiences and encounters, albethey masked in the whims of the Gods, history and the conundrums of fate, destiny and yes, a little fantasy.

CHAPTER 2

The Short Happy Life of Hạnh NGUYỄN

By

Hitoshi Iwashita

"Goddamn it. I did it, but I didn't mean to," Quy murmured to himself in the living room of his humble house in Hoi An.

He was staring at the tiny screen of his iPhone reading a short text from Hanh, a young, 16 year old girl that Quy had somehow got along with and she had become pregnant. He looked up, staring blankly at the ceiling, and sighed loudly enough for his daughter to notice and look over.

"Ba oi, are you okay?" asked his daughter.

"Ah con, it looks like it will soon be raining cats and dogs," replied Quy.

"Oh, I better take the laundry back in," said the daughter, rushing out to the small garden where all the laundry was hanging.

After she left, Quy took a deep breath and once again looked back at the screen, getting what the text meant to him. He recalled the meeting with her, the one which probably caused the pregnancy. That was exactly one and a half months ago. As usual, they had met in the rice field. She is a high school student and was working to help her family at a local market in Hoi An. Gradually, a sense of anxiety come up within his body, making him feeling bad. With a trembling index finger, he texted back "Let's meet up at the usual place tomorrow."

Quy looked up once again and thought about her. His daughter was busy taking in the laundry and folding the clothes. Outside it was getting darker and was almost 8 pm on a Friday. His daughter came back to the living room and started to fold the laundry on another couch while watching a local TV program. It was the usual way that he and his family of two daughters spent their evenings.

"I'm going to take a short walk," said Quy standing up from the sofa.

"At this late time? Oh, you don't look good by the way. Are you alright?" asked the daughter.

"I am fine. I just want to take a walk for change."

He went out of the room and through an alley behind his house. As he was walking down the alley, he ran into his neighbor Kim, a single mother and a local restaurant owner, who quickly spotted him.

"Anh Oi, did you hear all that last night? The couple on the corner argued and violently fought. They shouted at each other and even threw glasses! The argument was about their kids and housework..... They are so emotional and touchy. It was quite annoying," gossiped Kim with a mixture of a grin and smile on her face and not looking at all annoyed. Instead, she looked quite joyful and energetic.

"Oh well, sorry to hear about that. I did not know..... I slept like a dog last night," replied Quy.

"Ah ha, well, I may have a word with them. Hope they solved the argument. By the way, where are you going? I can go with you if you just want to hang around here," said Kim, leaning in towards him full of curiosity. She took his forearm as if they were a couple.

Quy just smiled back, gently took her hand away, politely declined her offer, and walked away. Kim raised her voice on his back, "So you are going to meet a girl, ha?" Quy kept walking while shrugging his shoulders.

In this local village, everyone knows every single event happening daily because the people love to gossip so much. Kim is at the center of all the gossip groups and is the most well-known gossip maker in the village. She is so friendly and curious to know every single event and everything that happens in the alley. Yet, nobody hates her on account of her friendly attitude and nice smile. The locals say that whenever anyone is feeling bored, they should go talk to her. She is very amusing even though she is sharing her often bad-mouthed opinions behind other people's back. Somehow, there are no hard feelings.

Quy is an old man. He is 63 years old and living in a village near Hoi An, a popular tourist destination in central Vietnam. He was born in Hoi An but is of Japanese descent with a Japanese father and a half Vietnamese mother. The father was a former soldier during the Japanese occupation in Vietnam from 1940 to 1945 during World War II while his mother was Japanese Vietnamese. She was an ancestor of the Japanese who were part of the construction of the Japanese Bridge in Hoi An. Quy was raised as a Vietnamese but his upbringing was also mixed with Japanese culture. He was lucky enough to be highly educated. He went to study at the University of London, Goldsmiths, in the UK on a government sponsorship. When he was in England, he became enthusiastic about reading English literature. Later on, he became an academic researcher at the University of Da Nang when he returned to Vietnam. He can speak multiple languages. He speaks English and Japanese very fluently, in addition to his native Vietnamese.

He looks skinny, but he is quite fit with a well-built body from doing daily exercises and doing Japanese martial arts every day which is something his father taught him when he was young. His hair has turned shining grey and his height is around 175 cm, a bit taller than an average man in Vietnam. He has Japanese blood and his look is somewhat non-Vietnamese, such as lighter skin and bright eyes. This has sometimes helped him to get acquainted with strangers pretty easily. He got married and had two daughters. He makes ends meet by operating his own travel agency that focuses on tourists from Asia and the West. These days he had become quite lonely because his wife passed away and he had also retired from his academic job. The tourist guide job was a way to pass the time while earning a bit of money.

He met Hanh because of this job. He guided a group of tourists to the wet market in Hoi An where Hanh works. Her family sells fresh local fruits to locals and tourists. As usual in Vietnam, there is never a fixed market price unless the customers know the seller well. Otherwise, without exception, the price is negotiated and foreigners almost always get overcharged, usually more than double what the locals pay.

One day, a Japanese tourist came to Quy to ask about the price of durian. This is called the King of Fruits because of its rich flavor which is like condensed cream.

"How much do you think it costs?" the tourist asked Quy showing him a 100-gram durian.

"Oh, durian! Well, you must have a good eye in the market. It should cost around five USD, I suppose," answered Quy.

"Er... I paid 40 USD," the Japanese said with disappointing frown.

"Ah, that is high, way high, too much, indeed. Well, let me re-negotiate with them," Quy quickly answered since he was responsible for having his customers feeling happy on the tour.

They went back to the seller in the market and that's when Quy met a young girl named Hanh for the first time.

"Em oi. It's nice to meet you. I am a tour guide. About the durian this guy bought, don't you think you charged too much?" Quy asked Hanh politely in English.

"Well, it's the market price," replied Hanh in broken Japanese.

Quy repeated his question in Japanese. Hanh kept staring at him.

Then, he repeated it once again, but in Vietnamese and added "I will no longer send you tourists unless you give him a discount."

Astonished, Hanh opened her eyes slightly more widely and then quickly smiled. She paid back half of 40 USD to the customer.

"You speak languages very good?" Hanh asked him full of curiosity while running her fingers through the silky long hairs in front of her face.

"Yes, I just studied from my family and at university."

"I wish I could speak better," replied Hanh making eye contact directly into his eyes.

"You can teach me sometime. I would like to learn," she continued.

"Sure, if you are nice to my customers, then I will."

Strangely enough, for Quy, she looked not only cute but attractive even though she was still a child. She wore colorful pajamas with red and yellow which is normal for a local market seller. She was skinny with long hair. Her neck and forearms revealed shiny white skin. Her eyes were cheerful and full of energy, and her body shape was well balanced, changing from a girl's body to a woman's body quite seamlessly. For Quy, she was not really attractive, but very pretty.

Hanh was born an orphan and then later on adopted by a local Vietnamese family when she was about 12 years old. The family were vendors at a wet market in the center of Hoi An. It was always filled with tourists. When at home, she tended to feel like an outsider with her foster parents and their two young daughters, one who was 12 and the other was eight years old. The adoptive parents treated her harshly while the other daughters were treated very well. In particular, the step father blamed almost everything on her. One day, he came home drunk and smacked her without reason and the others did not try to stop him at all. Soon he became tired of hitting her and went to bed, falling asleep instantly. Since then, he often hit her whenever he felt grumpy, even in front of others, which made Hanh really miserable. She did not want any trouble so she pretended to be obedient to the parents whenever talking to them. She patiently listened to their gossip about local issues and neighbors' quarrels though she became sick and tired of hearing such stories. She did not feel at home.

In the market, however, she enjoyed her time. She especially liked talking with strangers and tourists. In particular, she liked to talk to foreign tourists from Europe and Asia. She initially just observed and copied how other sellers talked to foreigners and how they made extra money. Then, she started to learn English, Chinese, and Japanese by watching dramas and comedies on YouTube. She had a good ear for learning languages and constantly practiced them with foreigners. Soon she learned how to make foreign tourists happy and have fun while making money and even raising prices to earn extra money. As she got to know Quy better, she appreciated his effort to bring all of his tourists to her shop. This became a main source of income for her family. The parents often traveled and left Hanh at home which actually made her very happy because she then felt free. The family's house was a small studio and they all sleep in the living room which was also the kitchen. By every weekend when the parent took days off, Hanh had become sleep deprived. In the very early mornings, her step parents tended to make love right next to the daughters and Hanh. Very often, the step mother would raise her voice and twist her body which made a wave in the bed and woke Hanh up.

Since knowing Quy, Hanh frequently bumped into him on the way home from the market because both lived in villages next to each other. One day, they bumped into each other as usual in the late afternoon after Quy had brought a group of European tourists to her shop. Hanh rushed to talk to him about a German tourist who had driven a hard bargain on fruits.

"Anh oi, what a day! He was so persistent and stingy!! He did not budge an inch for a dollar," said Hanh.

"Hmmm, that's right. Perhaps, it is something to do with nationality, the German people. They are well known for their stubborn character."

"But it was such a nice durian and all Europeans are rich, right? They could afford it!" replied Hanh grumpily.

They spent some time standing in the middle of the street before moving to the ditch as the bikes came along. They chatted about the nationalities and personalities of foreign tourists while sitting down together on the rice field hay and watching the sunset at twilight. Hanh and Quy found that they both loved watching the changes in the colors of the landscape, the reflecting ray of yellow sunlight on the walls of farmers houses scattered along the rice fields that changed into an orange and sometime purple color before going dark. It was before the harvest season and the rice fields were very quiet and peaceful.

After that first meeting, they started spending time together in the late afternoons. Quy found Hanh's energetic character interesting while she found his deep knowledge about European society and languages equally interesting. One day, they met once again and were chatting in the rice fields.

"What a relief today. The family left for Hue so I am alone at home. Hooray!" said Hanh with full smile.

The sounds of the breeze came off from the rice field and combined with the echoing voice of karaoke. The singer seemed to be badly drunk so he barely sang a song. Quy shook his head and smiled to Hanh, and she smiled back to him. All of sudden, Quy noticed her tearful eyes. He was a little confused, but gave her a hug. Hanh hugged him back tightly, and then Quy gently pushed her down into the hay bed. She did not resist at all and Quy did not miss her flirtatious smile lasting for a few seconds. Without hesitating, Quy slowly took her clothes off and entered her while she kept looking away. The love went quickly but Quy did not hear anything except her choppy sighs. After the love making, both kept laying down on the hay bed while hearing the sounds of the breeze mixed with karaoke from far. The moments were somewhat fruitful for both of them. It left Hanh feeling fulfilled and

Quy feeling good. Although neither of them noticed, Kim was quietly watching both as they were making love.

By March 2021, the international pandemic gradually impacted Vietnam. There were strict regulations for incoming foreigners and Vietnamese. As in other countries, the government started to promote a series of preventative measures such as washing hands, social distancing, and wearing masks. It also recommended working from home, rather than office work, so that people could not get infected in the workplace. It also adopted a strict lockdown which forced people to stay at home except for going shopping to buy daily essentials and seeing a doctor. There were still a few Covid patients identified, mostly foreigners and Vietnamese combing back from foreign countries.

After Quy received the text about the pregnancy, he arranged a meeting in the rice field as usual. The locals had started to be worried about Covid. They were talking about the possibility of having a curfew just like during the war. Quy still remembered the terrified experiences back in those days.

"Con oi, do you know if we have a curfew?" Quy asked his daughter.

"Ba, I really don't know! I hope there's no curfew," she answered. She was just too busy to do housework.

"Well, we have to be very careful with the police. They are hungry," said Quy.

"They are already patrolling around giving warnings to those who do not wear masks," answered the daughter.

"You know what? They are always trying to seize a chance to steal petty cash from good citizens like me. Well. They call a bribe a contribution. Contribution to what? To help their family via bribes? What the fuck is that? They are such bastards!" Quy gradually raised his voice and in the end was shouting in anger.

"Ba, I know that story. You told me more than a few times."

Like those in other parts of Vietnam, the police offices in Hoi An are notoriously eager to get bribes. Their salaries are quite low and those interrogated by them are encouraged to a pay to avoid trouble making it a win-win relationship between the locals and the police. Indeed, Quy had bad experiences with the police for some traffic accident before so he was very conscious about the police. He was wondering how much they would charge him if they knew he had made an underage girl pregnant. He still remembers the notorious faces of the police, whom he often saw on the streets of Hoi An.

The next day Quy was taking a walk while considering what to do about the pregnancy. For him, the people wearing masks looked unfamiliar and even very strange in such hot weather. It was in the middle of the dry season with glaring sunlight covering Hoi An from a complete blue sky with no clouds.

On the way back home, Quy bumped into Kim.

"Anh oi! An old yet hot man here! Where have you been? I saw a girl with you, ha? I think she is working at the local market, right?" asked Kim full of curiosity and with her usual smile.

"Ah... kind of," Quy replied with embarrassment.

"Ah ha, I know her for sure! Recently she seems to look very healthy even more than before... her rosy cheeks, being curvy, and looking more like a woman than a child, I think."

"Yeah, can be."

"You know what? I was like her before, a long time ago when I was a school girl. Can you imagine that?"

"Well, you still look a school girl, Em!" replied Quy, saying in his mind that I meant your childish habit of gossiping.

That night Quy had trouble sleeping well due to worrying about the likely bad consequences of the pregnancy. In Vietnam, having sexual relationships with a 16-year old is an illegal act. It is like child abuse. Indeed, Hanh is still a 16-year old which means that Quy can be sentenced to jail for up to 20 years. He knew he was old and did not think he could survive such an imprisonment. In exchange for a relatively big amount of cash to the police, he might be able to avoid imprisonment but he knew that he did not have enough money. Worrying about that made him awake for a long time, but he eventually fell asleep late in the night.

The next day Quy arranged a meeting with Hanh at a place near the center of the rice field. Getting out of the house, Quy spotted Kim, the gossip lady, in the middle of telling of her kid about his study habits and sometimes yelling about it. Quy just glanced at her while saying, "Take it easy, Em." Kim glanced at him but immediately started shouting at her kid without replying to him. Quy was relieved to see her too busy to investigate his personal matters.

At the meeting place in the rice field, Hanh was already there when he arrived. She was sitting down on the ground and looking at her feet while waiting for him in vain. Quy approached her and said hello, but she did not even look up.

"How is everything, Em?"

She just glanced him and looked down again as she seemed to be deeply depressed.

"Em oi, I know this is something that made you so embarrassed. I am so sorry about that," said Quy softly and quietly.

Quy continued.

"I am fully responsible for that. Em, you are still legally underage, meaning that you cannot give birth here. So let us have an abortion."

Hanh quietly nodded without seeing him. She had remained silent from the beginning.

"I know, I know how you feel, Em. It is embarrassing, confusing, and annoying. What we should do is have an abortion. That's the only option remaining for us."

Feeling a sense of guilt, Quy got down on his knees and gave her a hug.

Quy heard someone talking nearby and froze still. Quy thought it might be the police or community patrols so he stayed on the ground. They were lying next to each other. He was sure the patrols were because of Covid when everyone was afraid.

They stayed laying down for quite some time. Quy felt like it was forever, but it turned out to be just a half hour from the time Quy arrived. The rice fields were getting green as the rice had begun to grow quickly after planting.

"Ok, so let me arrange the things in the next few weeks, I will tell you what to do, alright?"

Quy looked in the eyes of Hanh and made eye contact for the first time that day.

"I am scared," said Hanh while looking at her stomach which was slightly more curved than before.

"Nope. No need to be scared. Just do what I tell you to do, alright? Then, everything will be fine."

After a long hug, they made love as usual and then both left.

After he returned home, Quy got busy calling hospitals to make an appointment for the abortion. It was not easy to do it because they were becoming very sensitive to Covid patients which were gradually increasing in numbers at that time. Eventually, he got the appointment for the next month. It would be in July at a public hospital in Hoi An. He texted the appointment date to Hanh with relief.

On the day of the July 2021 appointment, he arrived early so he could make sure of the operation. The appointment was set for 1:00 pm but Hanh did not show up. By 1:30 Hanh had still not arrived so Quy started to call her. Her phone seemed to be cut off. At 2pm, he tried to ring her again and nobody answered. He started to feel uneasy with the fact that she did not show up. Finally at around 2:30pm, he received a text message from her. It said, 'I cannot go there."

"What the hell is this?" Quy murmured to himself. She does not know how hard it was to make this kind of the appointment at this time. The situation has turned more serious than before with the lock-downs and with putting up barricades where there are Covid patients identified. Around 3:00 pm, after countless calls and texts, he made an appointment with her to meet in the late afternoon in the rice field.

In the rice field, Hanh was already there when Quy showed up.

"Em oi, I phoned you so many times. The abortion needs to be rescheduled. What happened to you?" Quy almost yelled at Hanh. She made a little bit of a face, looking nervous, and then making a straight face right away.

"So please tell me why not? I thought we made up our minds last time," Quy said continuing to be upset. He repeated himself while Hanh kept silent.

"I simply cannot do this," murmured Hanh. Quy was biting his tongue and being silent while gradually raising his shoulders and hold-ing his breath.

"Em, we talked about that already. You are underage and it is legally impossible to have a baby," shouted Quy.

"It is simply impossible here. You know that. Did you talk about this to anybody? It is not allowed here."

"Anh, we do not need to kill it. Do we?' answered Hanh.

"Absolutely not. But what do we do after the birth? In the first place, there is no life yet! I do not have the money to raise it nor do you, right?" said Quy still upset and even irritated. "It is nonsense to think that way. It's wrong."

She was quiet once again and without looking him just said, "Maybe you are right."

"Ok, so let me arrange it once again sometime within a month. Literally, the deadline for the abortion is sometime in the next month. Do not make a mess about it! Please don't, Em."

Hanh now seemed to be the one who is calm, cool, and collected while Quy has become upset and anxious. On his way back home, the anxiety came up from the bottom of his stomach and was making him very uneasy and unwell. That Friday night, people were enjoying themselves with parties and karaoke but Quy could not hear the sound because of his growing fear of having trouble with the police and Vietnamese law.

In September 2021, he again arrived early for the appointment so he could make sure of the operation. In reality, this was the very last chance to get an abortion since it had been almost 24 weeks since Quy got notice of the pregnancy in April. The situation with Covid had become dire with a full lockdown which forced him to get several documents and approvals just to go outside and to the hospital. It had become a mad, mad, mad world, Quy thought. Why do I need to get approval just to go out for a walk?

The appointment was arranged for 1:00 in the afternoon at the same hospital. Again, Hanh did not show up nor did she text him. Quy was patiently waiting while feeling that something unexpected was going to happen, but without knowing what it could be.

At 1:30 pm, Quy received her text message saying only "See you later in the usual place." Looking at the message, he took some time to think about what it meant and came up with a number of questions and complaints while staring back at the phone, but he just texted back with an "Ok."

In the same rice field where they always met, Hanh was not there. Quy waited for half an hour, feeling himself powerless and like a useless old man. He eventually fell asleep on the hay bed and was later woken up by Hanh.

"Hey, what was wrong with you?" asked Quy rubbing his eyes.

"I don't need the operation."

"What? What did you say?"

"I said I don't want the operation," said Hanh quietly.

Looking back at her face to face, Quy just stared into her eyes with a puzzled face. What the heck is the girl saying, thought Quy. I had made best efforts to arrange everything during the lockdown and now she is making my effort useless. Feeling his anxiety coming up, Quy bit his tongue and just said, "Tell me why."

"I think it is simply wrong to remove something... something I have in my body."

"Oh dear, we talked about that again and again. It is hard to have a baby financially and legally. We talked about that a million times, right?"

Hanh took Quy's hands in hers.

"Anh oi, I thought this through over the past few months," said Hanh bending towards him and looking into his eyes with confidence. "It is unethical to remove something I have inside of me. It is just unnatural. It would be killing unnecessarily..... I am thinking what can be wrong with giving birth."

"Uh....... We talked about that already and I thought you agreed with me," murmured Quy to himself.,

"Uh uh," said Hanh slowly shaking her head two times as she continued. "As you said, it is something like you see the mud while I see stars but we're looking at the same thing," said Hanh clearly to him and added in Japanese "Muri, Zetai Muri" meaning impossible.

Listening to her decisive tone of voice, Quy looked down and tried to process what she said and the possible results it would cause.

"I cannot stop you then" said Quy with a tiny voice.

"Daijoyobu, Mondai Nai!" mentioned Hanh with a sing song voice in Japanese, meaning no problem.

On the way back to the village, Quy noticed the changes in the color of the fields from green to gold for the first time that day making him a bit mellow. He felt like an old man that was following a young girl's will rather than managing her. The breeze in the rice field was no longer healing him as it did before. He heard someone laughing out loud from a far, feeling that he is the one being laughed at. Looking in that direction, Quy saw Kim and her friends chatting while walking towards their home in the rice field.

Since her decision to give birth, they frequently met in their usual place in the rice field and they made love occasionally as they did before. After September 2021, the Covid pandemic got calmer and the lockdown was being lifted in Hoi An, but the travel restrictions were not. As time passed by, Quy felt that he wanted to do something to help her on account of not only his feeling responsible and guilty but also his being brought into her decision. He was slowly sharing her decision as part of his and starting to look forward to having a baby. It had been almost eight months since she got pregnant. In fact, Hanh's belly expanded and her complexion was very rosy as she wore maternity clothes and bigger pajamas.

In October 2022, the weather was getting milder and moving from the dry to the rainy season in Hoi An. Enjoying the comfortable breeze, they met in the usual place and chatted about her health as well as their businesses after the lock down. All of sudden, Hanh groaned with pain and bent over her body nearly to the ground.

"Em, are you alright?"

"Nope, I think it is coming," replied Hanh.

"Eh? It is too early. You still have more than a month"

Panicked, Quy stood up and looked around above the yellow rice paddy. He saw a woman coming. She turned out to be Kim who was on the way back from shopping.

"Oh, what a coincidence. Please come help her. She is giving birth now!"

Jumping with surprise, Kim ran to Hanh without asking why Quy was here. Kim calmly checked her and took off her underwear saying, "Ua, it is really coming now. See part of its head." Quy saw some hairs.

"Go get some water," Kim shouted at Quy to get him to do something. He went to an irrigation ditch which was filled with trash and oil and then went to the other ditches which also looked the same. He then decided to just get dirty water and brought some back to Hanh. He then kept standing by while watching Kim helping Hanh to give birth. After watching her struggle for a long time, a time Quy felt was infinite, the baby was born and crying loudly in the arms of Hanh. But Hanh kept bleeding so Kim passed the baby to Quy to attend to Hanh.

Quy looked at the baby. They both stared at each other for a while. The baby did not look away and Quy felt like he was looking at himself in the mirror. It was getting late, but he kept standing and holding the baby while Kim was trying to stop the bleeding. After the bleeding stopped, Quy passed the baby back to Hanh but kept looking at the baby laying in Hanh's arms. As it turned dark, a car came from behind and its headlight reflected onto the golden field, shining onto the mother and the baby for a second. Quy was immersed in the scene and felt he was seeing something sacred. He kept standing there and staring even after the shine of light from the car had gone away. Kim told them to bring the baby back to the village so they started walking towards his home. Quy started to notice and realize that the baby was premature. Hanh must have been exhausted, but she looked completely joyful while carrying and looking at the baby in her arms.

"Er. You look familiar, so familiar," said Kim with her filthy smile and giving the side eye to Quy and then back to the baby a couple of times.

"Yes, indeed. What a coincidence, ha?" answered Quy looking back to Hanh who walking behind them.

Quy could not look away from the baby. He felt it was so connected to him. Kim did not ask further and was just looking at the baby while walking back.

Arriving to his home, Quy brought Hanh and the baby into the living room where his two daughters were doing housework.

"This is Hanh and her baby. We have them tonight because... " said Quy as both daughters jumped for joy and immediately ran to the baby with big smiles.

"Wao, it is so cute and adorable, he needs to be cleaned though," claimed a daughter.

"It somewhat looks like dad," said the other daughter.

"Kim and I helped her. They are so exhausted and need help so they will be staying with us tonight."

Both daughters immediately started to sort things out. They started with taking care of Hanh, setting up a bed, and preparing the bathroom to clean her and the baby.

Hanh was fulfilled with joy and both Hanh and the baby looked united. Quy knew she must be exhausted and that she had bled heavily. Everybody there was immersed into the scene and the baby was in the center of the living room of the humble house in Hoi An. Even the baby seemed to enjoy the moment.

In the early morning of the next day, the family was awaked by the crying baby in the living room. Hanh had passed out and was breathing only faintly. The daughters called for an ambulance and they went together to the hospital with the baby. The baby was diagnosed as premature so both of them were hospitalized from that day on. A few days later, Quy was informed by a doctor that Hanh had passed away on account of infections caused by the dirty water and too much bleeding when giving birth.

After the incident, Quy got busy with numerous chores. He went to register the newborn baby with the local authorities as well as registering the death of Hanh. He also met Hanh's foster family to share the news about what had happened to her in the hospital and about the baby. He suggested that he would adopt it if the family would not or could not do so. They immediately agreed without questioning or complaining. For Quy, it seemed that the stepfather and mother were indifferent to Hanh and glad to hear that Quy was going to sort everything out. The meeting lasted less than 10 minutes. They barely opened the mouths expect to say, "OK, no problem" and 'yes' to Quy adopting the baby. On the way back to his home, Quy got shivers down his spine and thought about how hard Hanh's life had been with her family and how it was more difficult than she told him.

The baby stayed in the hospital for a while but was eventually discharged and sent to Quy's home. Strangely enough, none of the daughters asked why Quy adopted it. In front of his humble house, Kim was cuddling the baby. Neither noticed when Quy arrived, but then Kim saw Quy and took the little boy's hand and waved it towards Quy while saying "Ba oi." Quy gave back to Kim a dry laugh and then a full genuine smile to the baby.

"It is a pity that she is not here. Your mum should have lived longer than that," Kim said softly to the baby. Shoulder to shoulder, Quy looked at the baby with Kim.

"Well, in fact, look at other people, most people just exist... merely eating and sleeping. At least, she lived her life, albeit a relatively short, but happy life," said Quy. Kim did not seem to be listening. She was looking at the baby. Quy also looked into the wide opened eyes of the baby. Suddenly, the baby burst into tears.

"There, there. Sorry for your dad saying such stupid words," said Kim to the baby.

Quy suddenly noticed the twilight was gathering and the dim lights were reflecting on his house's wall. The memories of being with Hanh in the rice field came flooding back.

The End

Hitoshi Iwashita

Hitoshi Iwashita is an author with a great passion for finding and creating life changing stories from daily life. By living in Vietnam for more than five years, he has become enthusiastic about doing Zen Buddhist practices, which has helped him to focus on truly being present. He loves traveling, practicing martial arts, enjoying music, and writing.

*This story is a construction of fragmented ideas that emerged through the **Saigon Writers Club's** creative writing workshop as well as my historical and direct life experiences in Vietnam and other countries. I was inspired by some of Hemingway's work, Zen words, and Oscar Wilde's work. They all came together at one time in the middle of one of our writing sessions. I highly appreciate the **Saigon Writers Club** organizer, Sam, and other participants who unintentionally or willingly helped me to develop my story.*

CHAPTER 3

Cik Supi's Mandi Bunga

By

Suhaila Kasim

As the birds chirped outside the window, the sun rose over Kanchong Darat, a small village in rural Malaysia and home to Malays, Chinese, and Indians who lived together in harmony. Cik Supi, one of the matriarchs of the village, rubbed her face with her right palm to end the *subuh* prayer. She folded the *telekung*, the praying dress, and walked to the nearest window and opened it wide.

"Assalamualaikum," she said to the morning breeze that came in and chilled her face. She then walked to the dressing table and sat on the chair to look into the mirror and check the fine lines under her beautiful round eyes.

"How lah to get rid of you wrinkles?" she said talking to herself with a sigh. She softly massaged her oval, high-cheeked-boned face and dabbed face powder onto her fair, soft cheeks.

She drew a line of eyeliner on the tips of the eyelids of her black round eyes which highlighted her beauty. She took three pieces of *ylang* from a bowl on the dressing table and slipped it into her hair bun. The day before she had plucked a bowl of *ylang* from the tree which she planted years ago. She spread the rest of *ylang* on her bed and the smell spread all over her room. She went back to her dressing table, checked her face again, and, satisfied with her looks, she walked out of her bedroom.

Cik Supi, a single mother to eight children and well known for her skills as a traditional Malay wedding make-up artist, lived in the small village of Kanchong Darat. She lived on a plot of land in a traditional Malay designed house that she inherited from her late husband. The land was planted with coffee trees that fed Cik Supi and her family. She and her kids plucked the coffee beans to sell to the Chinese merchant who called her "*mak*" which is a common name used for mother in Bahasa.

The main activities of the village which contributed to the residents' livelihood was from growing coffee, domestic livestock, and vegetables. Most of the Malays are farmers, the Chinese run the small businesses, and the Indians work as rubber tappers on the rubber plantations that surround the village and are mostly owned by British companies.

The people of the neighborhood live in harmony, integrity, and re-spect to each other. Some are very close to each other like brothers and sisters. They help each other regardless of their race or skin color. They also share the same taste buds and enjoy eating *nasi lemak* for breakfast, drinking coffee at the Chinese Kopitiam, and chatting over a *roti canai* and *teh tarik* at the *Mamak* shop, the Indian Muslim coffee shop. *Roti canai* is a flat crispy bread normally eaten with light *dhal* curry and *teh tarik* is a thick milk tea sweetened with condensed milk and poured from up high until foam forms on the top of the glass.

Cik Supi was not only relying on selling coffee beans for her family's survival. She also trades the *songket*, a traditional Malay cloth embroidered with either gold or silver threads. A merchant from Terengganu, a state on the east coast of Malaysia, regularly visits Cik Supi and supplies her with their fine handmade *songkets* which Cik Supi uses for her customers wedding dresses or to resell to the ladies in the village. Cik Supi's character has made many people who surround her feel loved and cared for and so many of them call her *mak*. The *songket* merchant also calls Cik Supi *mak* and he cares for Cik Supi like his own mother.

"Tok, tok, tok," she knocks on the door of Khadijah and Kasim's room.

Khadijah and Kasim are the only children living with her now because her other six children already have their own families and are living away. "Wake up! wake up! *salat*! *salat*!" her loud and assertive voice enters their ear drums like lightning and awakens both of her children from their sleep. They stretch and crawl out slowly from their bed and make their move to the bathroom.

A moment later, Cik Supi continues to the little staircase and towards the kitchen. Her thin light body helped her to avoid the cranking sound from the wooden planks as she stepped on the wooden floor. As she was walking to the staircase, she glimpsed at the house pillar where a small calendar was hanging. It showed yesterday's date, Friday, 17 April 1970, so she tore off that day's page so the current day of Saturday, 18 April 1970 was visible.

As she stepped down to the kitchen, a little kitty came towards her "ala, ala, cute little Milo," she said to the little kitty. She rubbed the back of the little kitty and kissed her cheeks with love. She walked to the sink of the kitchen and started washing the dishes that were left from last night's supper.

"Klick, klick," came the sound of the unlatched bathroom door which notified Cik Supi that someone was coming out from the bathroom.

"What time are you going to Cik Rose's house?" Khadijah asked her mom as she came out from the bathroom after completing the *wuduk*, a simple cleaning ritual before performing her morning prayer.

"Probably around 8.00, but I will prepare breakfast and lunch for you all before I go there," Cik Supi replied to her daughter.

As Khadijah went out from the bathroom, Kasim who sat on the dining chair went into the bathroom leaving the little kitty looking at him with hope that Kasim would continue to rub her back. A few seconds later, there was the swoosh sound of water splashing on his body. Then, Kasim came out from the bathroom.

"Kasim, faster, later I want you to help me fill up the kerosine stove. I want to cook breakfast," Cik Supi said to Kasim as he climbed upstairs to perform his morning prayer.

"Okay *mak*," replied Kasim politely to his mother with a smile.

Cik Supi continued cooking, searching for onions and shallots from the basket under the shelves at the corner of the kitchen. She planned to make *nasi lemak* for breakfast and lunch for Khadijah and Kasim because she would be away later. She sliced an inch of ginger from its original root and soaked a full handful of dried chilies in hot water. As the chilies floated and the seeds subsided, she drained and crushed them with shallot and ginger. She crushed and ground everything with a *batu giling* until the texture had become very fine.

After Kasim completed his duty to God, he filled up the kerosine bottle of the stove and placed it at the center of the Butterfly brand two burner kerosene stove. Kasim then ensured that the kerosine reached the wick to ensure the wick will light the stove.

"Done," Kasim told Cik Supi after he completed his task.

"Thank you," Cik Supi replied with smile to him showing that she was satisfied.

She then placed a black bottom pot on the left side of butterfly stove and poured in a cup of coconut oil. The coconut oil was made from the backyard coconut tree. She then lit up the stove. As the oil started to heat up, she poured the chili blends into the hot cooking oil. She stirred it slowly and covered it with a metal lid. When the *sambal* was nearly cooked, she added anchovies and sliced onions and let it simmer.

When the *sambal* was properly cooked, she washed two cups of rice. She added slices of shallots, two garlics, an inch of ginger, two pieces of pandan leaves, a bit of salt and a cup of coconut milk to make a *nasi lemak*. She placed the pot on the stove and let it steam. While the rice was steaming and cooking, Cik Supi fried some ground nuts and cut some cucumber as garnishing for the *nasi lemak*. After 20 minutes, her *nasi lemak* was well cooked and she covered the rice pot with a metal lid. The aroma of *pandan* leaves and coconut milk went into her nostrils and made her tummy grumble with hunger.

When everything for the *nasi lemak* was completed, Cik Supi went up to her bedroom to get ready to go to the bride's house. This was where she would perform as a make-up artist for the bride as well as the wedding planner for her customer Aliya, Pak Ali and Cik Rose's daughter.

Pak Ali was a well-known man in the village. He was wealthy and owned a lot of land and rubber trees and coffee as well as a small grocery store next to the public primary school. He was also one of the few in the village who owned a car, a Ford Cortina. Owning a car was a kind of social status. It was considered a luxury item in the 1970s when Malaysia was in a transition from an agricultural to an industrialized country.

After a heavy cooking of *nasi lemak*, all her light touch-up that she put on after prayer and before she started cooking had melted away. Cik Supi went to the bathroom and washed her face. She went upstairs to her bedroom and straight to the wardrobe. She took out one red *kurung pesak gantung*, a traditional Malay costume and matched it with a red *batik sarung*, a traditional Malay skirt for the *kurung*. Today she will wear a red *kurung pesak gantung* to Aliya's wedding. Before she slipped into her *kurung,* she wiped her wet face with a white towel while checking her face in the mirror. It was her habit to always check her face every now and then when she felt inadequate. She then slipped into her *kurung* and put on her *sarung*. When she was completely dressed up, she applied some powder on her flawless face and put on some eyeliner at the tip of her eyelids. She also pressed her lips onto a sheet of Chinese red pulp paper to make them red as a pomegranate. She took two pieces of *ylang* flowers for her hair bun and grabbed the red *selendang* to cover her shoulders.

"Khadijah, Kasim, I am going to Pak Ali's house now ya. Breakfast is already on the table. Don't forget to cover it with the *tudung saji* after you all finished eating," Cik Supi told her kids.

Cik Supi went downstair from the main house. She slipped her feet into a pair of red *tekat* shoes, a traditional style sandal that covered her toes but left her heels bare. She then walked slowly along the main road to Pak Ali's house waving hello to a Chinese man who was walking to a *kopitian* and a Malay man who was returning from the mosque.

The Malays mostly lived on their own plots of land and each house was about 100 to 500 meters away from each other. The Chinese community, on the other hand, mostly lived in a Chinese area that was set up by anti-communists who controlled the area. Their homes were close together. The Indians mostly lived on the rubber estates where they worked.

Cik Supi couldn't ride a bicycle nor a motorbike so she walked everywhere. Some villagers could afford a car, but most traveled by bicycle or used public transport if they traveled far from the village. It was customary for Cik Supi to walk to her customer's place if the distance was near. Sometimes, her customers would pick her up if they were from outside the village

"Where are you going Cik Supi?' asked Mak Limah as she passed her *warung*.

"I'm going to Pak Ali's house. Today is Aliya's wedding. Didn't you get the invitation?"

"Oh, of course, I got the invitation, but isn't it too early to go now?" asked Mak Limah.

"I have to get Aliya ready before her special day and have loads of things to do," explained Cik Supi to Mak Limah who was always the curious type.

"Okay then, see you later at Pak Ali's house," Mak Limah.

Cik Supi continued walking. Her buttocks, which moved left and right in rhythm, attracted every pair of eyes that she passed. The *ylang* smell was very nice and made every head turn towards her with curiosity to find out who was the person that had such a beautiful smell.

She walked confidently and was full of hope. The earnings from her service as a wedding planner and wedding make-up artist would help her feed her children. The selling of coffee beans to Ah Hock, the coffee bean merchant, was the main income for her family to survive. She was thankful for her late husband who had passed down the inheritance of a plot of land with coffee trees for her. Besides selling the raw beans to Ah Hock, Cik Supi also made coffee powder and sold that to her regular customers and sometimes at the night market.

Ali, the owner of the *mamak* shop that was famous for its *rojak mamak*, a dish of shrimp fritters, bean curd, fried potatoes, and cucumbers mixed with groundnut spicy sauce was one of Cik Supi's favorites. Both Ah Hock and Ali had become Cik Supi's very close friends until Ah Hock called Cik Supi *mak*.

After about 20 minutes of walking, Cik Supi arrived to Pak Ali's house.

"Assalamualaikum," Cik Supi announced her arrival to the house owner.

"Waalaikumsalam Cik Supi," Cik Rose, Pak Ali's wife, replied from inside the house. "Come in please."

As a mother of the bride, Cik Rose looked very happy and proud that her daughter was getting married at the age of 20 years old. It showed that her daughter was well raised, behaved as a Malay lady should behave, and knew the traditions. She would be a good daughter-in-law, a dream for many future parents-in-law and her husband to be.

Cik Rose reached out and shook Cik Supi's hand while pressing her cheek to cheek. Along the way to Aliya's room, Cik Supi saw that several ladies were preparing the ingredients for the menu that they would be serving at the wedding ceremony. Cik Supi waved to them while giving everyone a *salam* greeting. The ladies who helped prepare the food for the wedding were the backbone of this wedding. Without them, the menu would not be ready for the guests to enjoy at the wedding ceremony. They were all working hand in hand to ensure the wedding would be a special and memorable day for Aliya as well as for all the guests who attended.

"Where is Aliya?" asked Cik Supi.

"She's in her room," replied Cik Rose pulling Cik Supi towards Aliya's room.

As Cik Supi entered Aliya's room, she saw Aliya sitting at her dressing table next to the bed. She was folding and re-folding a handkerchief in the palms of her hands. Aliya seemed nervous about all the preparations for the wedding.

"Hi Aliya. How are you?" Cik Supi greeted Aliya with a warm smile.

"Hi, Cik Supi. I am good. How are you?" Aliya replied in a happy, relieved voice when she saw Cik Supi enter her room. She grabbed Cik Supi in a tight hug which relieved her nervousness.

"I'm good, very good," replied Cik Supi.

"Is the flower water ready for the *mandi bunga*?" Cik Supi asked when freed from her hug. *Mandi bunga* is a traditional Malay bathing water. It contains flowers and normally there is a mix of 10 or more types of flowers. But for Cik Supi, she always required that there be 20 types of flowers for her *mandi bunga*.

"Oh, I am not sure who will prepare it for me," said Aliya covering her mouth with her fingers in aghast.

"Lah, I thought I reminded your mom last week to prepare the flowers for the *mandi bunga*. You should have known about that too," Cik Supi said in a serious tone since she had asked that it be done a week ago.

"Okay, okay, let me check with mak," said Aliya who was panicked.

"It's okay. You stay here while I check with your mom. Today is your day. Let others do things for you," Cik Supi tried to calm Aliya down as she left to find Cik Rose.

"Cik Rose, Ooo....Cik Rose" she called out glimpsing through the kitchen door.

"Yes, Cik Supi. Is there anything that I can do for you?" asked Cik Rose noting that Cik Supi seemed panicked.

"Cik Rose, have you prepared the water mixed with flowers for Aliya's *mandi bunga*?" asked Cik Supi.

"Yes, I did. It's in the bathroom," Cik Rose answered confidently to hopefully relieve Cik Supi's nervousness. She pulled Cik Supi to the bathroom where she had prepared the water mixed with flowers.

"Here it is as you wanted," Cik Rose showed her a pail of water mixed with Jasmine, Rose and Bougainville.

"Oh, no. This is not enough."

"Uh?, ...not enough? What is not enough?"

"The flowers! There are only three kinds of flowers here," Cik Supi half screamed in disappointment. "There needs to be 20 types of flowers and here there are just three. Where are the other 17 flowers?"

"Assalamualaikum. What the hell is going on? What's all this noise about?" interrupted Mak Limah who suddenly appeared in the kitchen door. The hot discussion about the flowers had attracted Mak Limah to the house.

They both returned the greeting, but Cik Rose was uncomfortable with an abrupt question from Mak Limah and Cik Supi making such a big fuss about the flowers. "Nothing serious," Cik Rose replied to Mak Limah.

"How can you say it is nothing serious Cik Rose? Don't you know that I will not proceed with makeup if the *mandi bunga* is not complete?" said Cik Supi.

"What? Twenty types of flowers for a *mandi bunga*!" Mak Limah responded uninvitedly. "Don't you know that the *mandi bunga* is *bid'ah*. It's a falsehood and forbidden in Islam, Cik Supi oi!"

"The *mandi bunga* is not *bid'ah*, Mak Limah. *Bid'ah* is when you ask from others rather than God or pretend to be God. That's *bid'ah*. The *mandi bunga* is only a practice of cleaning, refreshening, and to get a better smell for a special occasion."

"*Mandi bunga* is *sunnah*. Our *sunnah* actually encourages us to be clean, to freshen up and smell good. Don't you know that, Mak Limah? Our Prophet Muhammad p.u.h, was always clean and smelled good. So, as a good follower of our Prophet, don't you think we should always be clean and smell good like our Prophet by practicing the ritual of *mandi bunga*? And by the way, the flowers not only give off good smells, but they are like a therapy element that can help us to de-stress and relax," Cik Supi explained to Mak Limah.

Mak Limah felt offended about the explanation and still wanted to find a weakness in Cik Supi's response.

"But why must you hassle yourself just to find twenty types of flowers for bathing?" Mak Limah said with her eyes rolling while her mouth was chewing betel leaves. "And what's more, you read some spell on the water before you start bathing the bride, right? Isn't that like seeking help from the flowers?"

"Oh come on, Mak Limah. The more flowers you mix with the water, the better the water will smell. Please study before you make any more statements. I did not glorify or adore anything, except God. I will always start my ritual with '*Bismillahirrahmanirrahim*, In the name of Allah, the Most Gracious and The Most Merciful' and pray that God will always protect the bride from any harm and disease while making the bride look fresh for her special day. That's all," Cik Supi responded stressing her opinion to Mak Limah. "Don't you think it is a good ritual Cik Limah? I don't see anything wrong in getting clean, feeling fresher, and smelling better," Cik Supi continued with her defense while looking for someone to help her.

"Mat, Mat, come here," she called to Mat, the youngest son of Cik Rose and Pak Ali. Mat is 11 years old, a dark skinny boy with short black hair. He grinned when Cik Supi called him and he walked toward Cik Supi.

"Yes Cik Supi?"

"Mat, please get a few of your friends and find 17 different types of flowers for me. I want to make flower bath water for your sister. The *mandi bunga* needs 20 types of flowers and your mom only has three types of flowers so I need another 17 types of flowers to complete the *mandi bunga* or otherwise we cannot start the make up for the bride."

"Seventeen types of flowers?" Mat asked in a daze. "Where can I find that many flowers? That's too many."

"Why don't you ask your friends to help you? Ask them to go around this village and ask from every house. I believe each house has at least has one of these kinds of flowers," Cik Supi said giving Mat instructions on how to find the 17 types of flowers.

"Must it be 17? What if we cannot find that many?" asked Mat doubting that he and his friends could collect 17 types of flowers.

"Sure you can. You can get all 17 types of flowers if you follow my tips. Knock on every door in this village and collect as many flowers as you can from each of the houses. You probably will get more than I need," Cik Supi said confidently hoping that Mat will buy her words and bring her the 17 types of flowers.

While scratching his head which was not itchy, Mat just nodded and obeyed. "Ok, ok, I will try to find it." He left to look for his friends.

Mak Limah was astounded by Cik Supi's lengthy explanation so she walked straight to Aliya's room and asked Aliya, "Didn't you have your shower today? Why do you need to do *mandi bunga*? Isn't your bathing this morning sufficient for your special day? And by the way, do you believe in *mandi bunga* Aliya?" Mak Limah asked sarcastically to Aliya who was sitting on the edge of the heavy metal bed frame.

"I had my regular bath this morning Mak Limah, but I am looking forward to the *mandi bunga* because I feel tired and sweaty. I need to refresh my body and the flower water will help me to destress and I will feel relaxed as well as to remove my nervousness."

Mak Limah accepted Aliya's response. She then started rummaging through the delivery trays to check the cakes on each tray while commenting that the decorations on the cake were not done properly, the colors of the flowers were not a match, the cake color base was wrong, and other things. Aliya just rolled her eyes.

Mak Limah was in her mid-50s, fat, and a fair skinned lady who was close to menopause. She never had children, ran her own *warung*, a small traditional Malay coffee shop with her husband, and always lived in stress. She was never satisfied with anything and always annoyed anyone near her with her depressing behavior without her ever realizing it.

Aliya heard Mak Limah complaining to herself about the wedding cake, but she did not want to bother with her complaints. Instead, she got up from the edge of her bed and went to her dressing table. She opened the drawer of the dressing table and took out some mint candies and gave them to Mak Limah.

"Here are some sweets for you. I hope after you had them you will talk sweet rather than complain," quipped Alia to Mak Limah who squinted at her before walking out of the room towards the kitchen.

Mat went out from the main hall and walked to the guest tents. He waved to a small group of boys ranging in age from seven to 12 years old. They went to the same school and frequently played *konda kondi*, a traditional Malay game that has two teams. One team will dig up a stick and throw it as far as they could. The opponents will try to catch it. If they can catch the stick, they win and if they fail to catch the stick, they need to throw the stick as near possible to the mother stick (the stick used to dig up the smaller stick). They then count the distance of the throwing stick from the mother stick and points are calculated.

"Hey, friends come here," Mat called out to the group. They immediately went to Mat with curiosity. "Cik Supi is looking for flowers for the *mandi bunga* that she is preparing for my sister. She said she will not do the make-up for my sister if she does not bathe my sister with flower water for the *mandi bunga*. That means no wedding if she cannot perform the *mandi bunga*. So, I want you all to help me find the remaining 17 types of flowers for her *mandi bunga*. Can you do that?"

The boys seemed to have no choice but to help Mat to find the remaining 17 types of flowers for Aliya's *mandi bunga*. They all nodded in agreement.

"Thank you, friends," Mat grinned.

The boys divided themselves into three groups to find the 17 types of flowers that Cik Supi wanted. Each group had three or four members and went to separate parts of the village. One group went to the area of the village where the Indian community lived. Another went to the Malay section and the last group to the Chinese neighborhood. Each community had their own personal preferences for flowers which, the boys thought, would make it easier for them to collect many different types of flowers. The idea was to collect the flowers preferred by these three main communities since they all grew flowers for their traditional and religious rituals.

The Indian community was well known for their jasmine garlands that they normally used for weddings or gifts to their Gods at the temple. The jasmine garland normally had a mix of jasmine, spider lilies, red roses and marigolds and most Indian homes would have at least one of these types of flowers.

For the Chinese community, flowers are symbols of luck. Chinese roses, for example, are a symbol of good luck and are normally used to celebrate success and birthdays. Many Chinese families will plant roses in their gardens or backyards. The lotus flower in Buddhism means purity so some families planted lotus flowers in front of their homes. Orchids symbolized love, beauty, and wealth and so many young Chinese would have this flower indoors as part of their home decor. The Chinese also believed that chrysanthemum tea can relieve headaches and so these are planted for health benefits.

The Malay community believed that flowers provide good and fresh energy because of the fragrance they produce. Therefore, many Malays love to plant jasmine, ylang, and fragipani flowers for home and body fragrance as well as for cleaning rituals.

The boys headed out by bicycle and on foot towards their target homes and started knocking on doors. At the first door, an old man answered their knock.

"Ha... what do you want? Knocking on people's house?" asked an old man to the group of boys.

"Can we pluck some flowers from your garden? Cik Supi wants it for her *mandi bunga*," explained the tallest boy in the group.

"Oh..... ok , you can but just don't clean it all out. Leave some!"

The boys nodded and went to old man's compound to search for the flowers and plucked few from each type that the old man had planted around his house.

On the other side of the village, another group of boys did the same thing.

"Assalamualaikum, Mak Wan, OOOO..... Mak Wan," said the smallest boy in the other group.

"Waalaikumsalam. Who is that?" Mak Wan walked towards the door and gave the salam greetings.

"I'm Lan, Mak Wan," the little boy introduced himself.

"Ohhh.... Lan, what is it?"

"Mak Wan, can we pluck some flowers from your garden?"

"What do you want to do with the flowers?" Mak Wan asked.

"Cik Supi is preparing water for a *mandi bunga* for Kak Aliya so we are searching for flowers for her."

"Ohhh for a *mandi bunga*. Ok, ok, take as many as you want."

"It's good that you come and pluck all these flowers now. Later on, they will be replaced with a new bloom," Mak Wan said happily. She was also grateful that it would reduce her work load when the dry flowers fell to the ground.

"Thank you, Mak Wan," said Lan grinning happily. He could see nearly 10 types of flowers surrounding Mak Wan's garden. The boys happily plucked roses, lilies, hibiscus, magnolia, sunflower, azalea, jasmine and aster flowers.

After more than an hour of the boys going from garden to garden and from house to house picking flowers, they returned to gather in front of Pak Ali's house.

"Mat, these are all the flowers that we managed to collect," one of the boys said.

"Let's count how many flowers we have," Mat said to the boys. "Put them all here on the mat and arrange them in the same group of flowers." The boys arranged the flowers they collected on the mat by group and in rows.

"Ok, one, two, three, four, five, six, seven, eight, nine, ten, eleven, twelve, thirteen, fourteen, fifteen and sixteen, ermmm... this is not enough, we need seventeen," Mat counted the flowers again and realized that the flowers were not sufficient for the *mandi bunga* as requested by Cik Supi. All the boys scratched their heads even though none had an itch.

"Where else can we find them? We went to most of the houses in this village and collected most of flowers they had in their gardens and backyard," explained the tallest boy in the group.

"One more. Just one more," Mat said to the boys. "Do you know what flowers we need to complete this to 17? It's a kind of orchid."

The tiniest boy in the group shouted, "Ha! I know. Mak Limah has that orchid in her house. Maybe we can ask her to give the orchid to us."

"How do you know that? How dare you enter her home," Mat said.

Mak Limah's house was the only house that the boys did not dare to go to even though they knew Mak Limah was at Pak Ali's house. Her husband was also out, but only the smallest boy dared to peek through a gap in Mak Limah's window and saw an orchid on the side table.

"Mak Limah is at Pak Ali's house. How could she know that someone entered her courtyard?" the smallest boy said with pride to Mat.

"Ish, do you think she would give it to us? That's her special orchid and that's why she kept it inside her house," Mat told the boys.

"If we never try, we will never know," said one of the boys with darker skin than the others.

"Who dares to see her and ask? She's there in the kitchen. Go ask her," the tallest boy told the boys.

"Let me try," replied Mat.

"Put the shallots and onions on the corner. It will be easier to grind them together with the chilies," instructed Mak Limah to one of the ladies who was washing the shallots and onions.

"Okay Mak Limah," the lady nodded and put the basket full of shallots at the corner where the grinder was next to the basket full of chilies.

"Mak Limah, oooo Mak Limah," Mat called out.

"Yes Mat, what do you want boy?"

"Mak Limah, can you give me the special orchid that you keep in your house?"

"What?!!! What did you say?" Mak Limah half screamed.

"It is like this Mak Limah. Cik Supi asked us to find flowers for Kak Aliya's *mandi bunga* but we are short just one type of flower to complete Cik Supi's requirement of 20 different types of flowers. Mak already had three flowers and we found 16 more flowers so we're short just one kind."

"Ehh? No, no, no way. I will not be part of the *bid'ah* and sin action....
NO WAY!" Mak Limah strongly declined Mat's request for her orchid
while waving her pointed finger directly at Mat's eyes and nose.

"But.... Mak Limah....pleaseeee... we need just one more flower."

"SORRYYYY..... over my dead body. I will never give my favorite
orchid to you and that's final."

"Uhhh......ok then," Mat was disappointed with Mak Limah's decision and walked lazily back to his friends.

The boys were waiting for Mat with hope. They thought he could
manage to convince Mak Limah to give her orchids to them. But from
afar they saw Mat shaking his head to the boys signaling that his efforts
had failed.

The boys were sitting helplessly in front of the flowers that they had
gathered when Cik Supi suddenly appeared.

"Hey boys. Have you got all the flowers that I wanted?"

The boys were uneasily looking at each other and answered to Cik
Supi confidently, "YESSS... we did."

"Let me see what you all got for me," Cik Supi replied happily as she
started to count. "Eh, sixteen? This is not enough. We need one more
flower, boys."

"Ya we know, but can you just proceed with these?" Mat asked
hoping that Cik Supi will just proceed with the *mandi bunga* with the
flowers that they had.

"Cannot, cannot. It must be 20 flowers. Otherwise, it is not a proper *mandi bunga*," Cik Supi insisted.

The boys all started scratching their heads and looking at each other pointlessly. "But how?" asked one of the boys.

"I don't care. You all must get one more flower for me to prepare the *mandi bunga*, quickly, otherwise I will not proceed with the *mandi bunga* for your sister Aliya and it will delay her wedding."

Pak Ali was observing the boys and Cik Supi from the guest tent and was curious about what was going on because both Cik Supi and the boys looked so tense. He walked over to them and asked, "What are you all worried about?"

"We are short one type of flower for the *mandi bunga*. I asked the boys to get the flowers for me but we're still short of one type of flower and I will not proceed with a *mandi bunga* for Aliya if the water is not mixed with 20 types of flowers. Now we have 19 types of flowers and still need one more."

"Ahhh..... the *mandi bunga*. Is it compulsory to have 20 types of flowers?" asked Pak Ali.

"Of course. For me, 20 types of flowers are a must for the *mandi bunga* that I prepare. Otherwise, it's just a waste."

"That's your personal requirement, but not the *sunnah*'s requirement," Pak Ali sighed and clarified what is needed and what is not in Islamic practice.

"Ermmm... ya, of course it is not *sunnah* to have 20 types of flowers but it's better to have more than just a little to have a good effect for Aliya."

"That's when you look at the extreme benefit, but the *sunnah* says that we should be simple and an average amount of flowers is sufficient. The *sunnah* also does not encourage to do things that cause a burden to you or others," Pak Ali poignantly explained to Cik Supi.

She couldn't deny this, but had to admit and accept what Pak Ali was saying was true.

"Ok lah, I will proceed with the *mandi bunga* for Aliya."

"That's the spirit!" Pak Ali grinned and made his move towards the guest tent to set up tables for dining during the wedding.

"Thank you, boys, for your help," Cik Supi said to the boys as she put all the flowers collected by them into a big basket and moved it all to the bathroom where she removed every petal from each of the flower stems, cleaned the flowers, and rinsed them. After all the petals had been removed, she recited, "Bismillahhirahmanirrahim" and added all the petals into a big pail of water. The fragrance from each of the flowers spread all over the bathroom. She then took the *mandi bunga* to Aliya's room.

"Aliya, come bring your towel and *batik sarung* to the bathroom. The flower water for the *mandi bunga* is ready. The faster you take the *mandi bunga* the earlier I can put on your make-up," urged Cik Supi to Aliya.

Without hesitating, Aliya agreed. "Yes, Cik Supi, I am coming now. Thanks for the flower water and for the *mandi bunga*."

In the bathroom, Cik Supi asked Aliya to take off her clothes and put on the *batik sarung* covering her chest and tied at the bosom. Aliya then sat on the stool beside the *kolah*. With a "Bismillahirrahminirrahim" prayer that Cik Supi recited in her heart, she poured the cold water on top of Aliya's head. Aliya felt the water covering her head and pouring down all over her body wetting the *batik sarung* and exposing her feminine figure. After the third pour, Cik Supi untied the *batik sarung* and let Aliya hold part of the edge of it to avoid it from falling down and uncovering her whole body. She just wanted to loosen the *batik sarung* from Aliya's body to allow her to rub and clean Aliya's back. After Aliya was clean and satisfied, Cik Supi asked her to dry her body with the towel. A few minutes later, Cik Supi passed Aliya a new dry *batik sarung* to cover herself.

"Thanks, Cik Supi," Aliya opened the bathroom door and took the *batik sarung* from Cik Supi's hand. She covered herself and went out of the bathroom to her bedroom happily because she felt so clean and refreshed. She also felt a new sense of energy coming into her body. The nice flowery fragrance helped eliminate the tense and nervous feeling that had been occupying her mind. She was now happy.

Mak Limah who was in the kitchen saw both Cik Supi and Aliya coming out from the bathroom and she felt uneasy and began looking curiously at them. She left the basket of shallots on the floor and walked towards Cik Supi and Aliya.

"Cik Supi, Aliyah, wait a minute," she called out. They heard Mak Limah's voice and stopped their step immediately.

"Ya Mak Limah, what is it? What can I do for you?" asked Aliya. "Is there any important thing that you want to know or us to know?"

"Nothing. I was just wondering if you finally did the *mandi bunga* or not."

"Yes, we did finally, Mak Limah. I feel fresh now," Aliya grinned in response.

"Oh, I thought you will not proceed with a *mandi bunga* if you did not get the last flower to complete your 20 flowers. Right, Cik Supi?" Mak Limah knew that Cik Supi was insistent on having 20 flowers for the *mandi bunga* and she knew that she was short of one flower.

"Yes, I proceeded with the *mandi bunga* even though I was short one of the flowers. Pak Ali advised us to proceed. It's true that the number of flowers is not so important. What is important is the *sunnah* to get clean and fresh. With less than 20 flowers, the water still gives the benefits from the mix of flowers soaked into it and can still provide the same affects to Aliya. The most important thing is Aliya is satisfied and she feels clean, fresh and at ease."

"Ah, I see and understood now," Mak Limah admitted with satisfaction. "Ok lah, go on. I just want to know about that. I also want to continue my cooking at the kitchen."

Both Cik Supi and Aliya continued walking to Aliya's room. As they entered the room, Aliya uncovered the towel from her shoulders and put it on the bed and then sat down on the chair. Cik Supi let Aliya get seated comfortably then opened her make-up bag. She then started to put make-up on Aliya's face.

First though, she recited "Bismillahirrahmanirrahim" and in her heart she prayed for all good things for Aliya. She hoped that God will help Aliya to look good on her special day and protect her from anything that might harm her and her groom as well as her family. She then plucked a few of Aliya's eyebrow just to get her a fine line of eyebrow so the eyebrows would look neat. After she was satisfied with the eyebrow line, Cik Supi started applying powder thoroughly on to Aliya's face. She then carefully made a fine line at the edge of Aliya's eyelids with eyeliner. She drew on Aliya's eyelids and checked and rechecked again her work. She was satisfied.

She then put a piece of Chinese red pulp paper in between Aliya's lips and asked her to press her lips together. Seconds later, Aliya's lips became red like an apple. Cik Supi checked Aliya's look for a final time and was satisfied with color of Aliya's lips, the line she drew on Aliya's eyelids, and the thickness of powder that she put on Aliya's face. Now she moved on to do Aliya's hair. Cik Supi made a very nice hair bun and placed a traditional Malay head gear like a crown made from brass on Aliya's head. She added a single *sanggul goyang*, a traditional Malay hair pin made from brass that has flower motifs at the end of the pin and the flower looks like it is dangling from the end of the pin. This made Aliya look like a Malay queen. When she was done with the makeup, Cik Supi asked Aliya to uncover herself from her *batik sarung* tied at the bosom and asked her to put on the *kebaya songket*, the Malay traditional costume made from a cloth woven with gold thread flower motif that she had placed on the bed.

Aliya put on the red *kebaya songket* with its spread of gold flower motifs on her body. Cik Supi helped her to fit into the top. The traditional Malay *kebaya* came in two basic pieces, one on top and the *sarung* on the bottom part of the skirt. As an accessory, Cik Supi put on a *selendang* on Aliya's shoulders and across her body. The *selendang* is a piece of cloth like a scarf that is placed on one of the shoulders and crosses the body. As Aliya completed her *kebaya* wearing, Cik Supi put on Aliya's original gold jewelry, the necklace, the bracelet and her engagement ring. Cik Supi also added some fake gold accessories like long fake gold necklaces and bracelets to make Aliya look like a real queen who was covered in luxury. With Cik Supi's duty as a make up artist for the traditional Malay bride completed, both smiled in satisfaction.

"Ok, now you are ready Aliya," Cik Supi said with pride.

Aliya smiled ear to ear and thanked Cik Supi while hugging her happily. She then sat on the dressing table chair. The One-day Queen couldn't wait to see her One-day King for the solemnization moment.

Cik Supi smiled in satisfaction when she looked at Aliya. She felt proud of herself that she had made someone beautiful and look like a queen and had made the One-day Queen feel happy too. "Ok Aliya, sit and relax ya," she said. "I want to go out and check whether the groom is here or not."

Cik Supi walked out of Aliya's room towards the main hall where the bridal dais was set up. As she entered the main hall, she saw that the guests had started taking their seats. Cik Supi then saw the groom who looked handsome in his *baju melayu songket*, a traditional Malay costume for men made from *songket* with *tengkolok*, a traditional Malay head gear for men. He was walking towards a big cushion placed in front of the bridal dais where the solemnization process would take place. As the groom seated himself on the cushion, Cik Supi saw the Qadhi enter the hall. This was a Muslim man in charge of Islamic customary Shariah Law who would do the *akad*, the Islamic marriage contract. Cik Supi quickly made her move to Aliya's room to get her ready for the solemnization ceremony.

"Aliya, Aliya, get ready. Your One-day King is here and everybody is sitting down," Cik Supi excitedly informed Aliya who just sat quietly but was smiling ear to ear.

A moment later, Pak Ali entered Aliya's room and he looked proudly at his daughter. Even though it was hard for him to let Aliya go to her future husband, he was happy that today will be the most memorable moment for Aliya.

"Are you ready Aliya?" asked Pak Ali.

A moment later, Cik Rose entered Aliya's room to get her ready to be escorted to the bridal dais for the solemnization course.

"Yes, Abah," Aliya nodded to her father signaling to him that she was now ready.

Cik Rose escorted Aliya to the bridal dais followed by Pak Ali. Cik Supi also walked beside Aliya to ensure that Aliya looked right in her traditional costume. When Aliya was seated at the bridal dais with her mother beside her, the solemnization process started and was completed in just an hour. Aliya and her groom were now officially pronounced as husband and wife. Cik Rose and Pak Ali were soaked in happy tears and they hugged each other. That moment touched everyone's heart who witnessed the solemnization of Aliya and her husband.

Cik Supi tears dropped onto the cheeks of her fair skin. She was happy and proud that despite the shortages and hurdles in the process of preparing Aliya as a bride, she had finally made the bride, the groom, and the parents happy.

Mak Limah who had been in the kitchen for hours stood beside Cik Supi to witness the solemnization. When it was complete, she was so happy that she suddenly hugged Cik Supi unintentionally. Mak Limah looked deep into Cik Supi's eyes and said, "Congratulations Cik Supi. You have made Aliya looks like a queen today."

Cik Supi smiled back and said, "Thank you Mak Limah."

She was surprised that Mak Limah had hugged her and congratulated her despite her criticism about the *mandi bunga*. Now, though, both were happy as well as Aliya's parents.

Cik Supi and Mak Limah walk hand in hand out of the main hall.

The End

Suhaila Kasim

Suhaila Kasim is a Malaysian housewife living in Ho Chi Minh City, Vietnam who has passion for painting, crocheting, and quilting. Having left her career back in Malaysia, she has tried to explore and find activities that could become a therapy for her from being stressed out about not doing anything at home and being lonely while everyone else goes to work and school. Writing is one of these therapies. It also allows her to express herself and share what she likes with others. After nearly eight years of living in Ho Chi Minh City, she has managed to earn her master's degree in management and has explored her own talent in painting, crocheting, quilting and most importantly in writing. Cik Supi's Mandi Bunga is her second attempt to write a short story, but the first time she will be published.

This story is inspired by the life of my late grandmother who was a single parent and raised eight kids. Living a simple life and having a spirit that contributed to the community made many in the village respect her and made her well known amongst the community at that time. Her life has always inspired me to be an independent woman and believe that no matter who we are there's always "rezeki"(a Malaysian word borrowed from Arabic that means 'sustenance') for us and there's always a way to live happily and comfortably as long as we always remember that God is always with us and that we do everything with love and passion.

CHAPTER 4

Memo From the Landlord

By

Sam Korsmoe

I tell 'ya, I've been doing this for a while and I'm still amazed by the power of little kids. It doesn't seem to matter how old they are. They can be infants, just a couple weeks old, and they make a face or eye contact, grab a finger in their fat little fists, burp, sneeze, or fart and everyone in the room goes bat shit crazy.

It's usually funny, but it can also be quite profound. The profound part happens when they get older, like say around six or eight years old. It happens again when the kids aren't really kids anymore, but teenagers which is when guys like me have to get back on the job in a big way because some of them lose their way. It can get messy, but their impact power is definitely still there.

The little ones though never lose their way. Well, I shouldn't say *never* because some of them do, but if they have someone in their corner who loves them unconditionally, they just go on about their way. That's when it's fun to watch. That's when their influence reaches the profound.

In my last gig, I got a bit too committed with a couple of my kids. We're not supposed to do that, but, hey, I'm really the same as anyone else, at least where it counts on the inside. Besides, it all makes for a really good story that I've been wanting to tell for a long time. And now I get to tell it.

In early 2017, I was assigned to be the editor of a daily newspaper in southwest Montana. My guy was one of the reporters and he covered politics on the Montana and national affairs desk. He had an eight year old son. It was just the two of them. For whatever reason, I have a soft spot in my heart for single dads. I think overall there are probably more single moms, but they already get lots of attention (and many of them need it) while the dads generally don't. I'm pretty good with them which is maybe why I got this assignment.

Anyway, this particular dad, his name is Max S and his boy's name is Colin, was having some trouble adjusting to life in 2017. That's when I showed up. It was a couple months after the inauguration of a new US president.

"Max, can you drop by for a sec? We need to talk about your piece," I said over the intercom phone in our newsroom.

We're a medium sized daily newspaper with pretty good reach across all of Montana and a bit into Idaho and Wyoming. Max's stuff is really good. A lot of people read his articles and now and then I ask him to write a column for the op-ed page which generates a ton of letters to me and most of them are positive. Lately, though, he seems to be in a downward spiral.

"Be right there," he answers.

I watch him hang up the phone and start walking across the newsroom to my office. He's stressed out. I can tell. I can see it. He's slumped over with a few days' growth of beard on his face. He looks like he's been crying because his eyes are red either from a lack of sleep or maybe he actually has been crying. I've already seen that a few times. His clothes are rumpled too, more than normal. He's never really paid attention to clothes, but even less so over the past few months. Something is up, and I pretty much know what it is.

"What's going on?" he says as he plops down into a chair in front of my desk.

"Your piece on public lands. I'm not sure we should use the words, and I quote, "stupid fuckwit" in the lead paragraph. Kinda strong don't you think?"

"Well, he is. That EO will grant rich fucks the right to gate off access to public lands just because a public road happens to cross their private land. This is a public lands access issue that has been settled for a hundred fucking years. He can't just let them put up gates because they don't want to let poor people cross their land. That's illegal."

"And I get it. Just report on the Executive Order. Interview some private landowners and get their reaction to the EO. Talk to the wildlife and conservation groups. They're all up in arms and have already started filing lawsuits. What the hell. Talk to some lawyers. There's a process here, man, and our job is to report on it."

Over the past few months, this same conversation has played itself out numerous times on a variety of issues. Journalists are hardly saints. They throw F-bombs around all the time, but this time it's different. Max never really did that too often and he was usually quite happy with life, but that was before the 2016 American election. Since then, so many people around Montana and around the country suddenly started to hate each other and everything around them. Unfortunately, Max's job was to report on the issues that drummed up the hate and it was getting to him.

As usual, I convinced him to re-work the lead and focus the piece on the conservation groups' lawsuits against the EO that the new president signed. Max is a pro. All the 'fake news' bullshit that gets thrown at him bounces off. It's not that. He still does his job, but he knows that he's pushing it and he knew that I would call him on the stupid fuckwit thing. The problem is he keeps doing it and short of firing him I'm not too sure what to do. I can't fire him though, or at least I won't, but someone above me might. We're not all powerful, you know, and I still have to follow local rules.

As we were talking, I see his face suddenly light up when he looked out into the newsroom. The reason I can't fire him had just walked through the door. It's Colin, his eight-year-old boy who's in the third grade. Max's eyes lit up and a smile started to form on his face. He excused himself with his standard phrase of 'I'll take care of the piece' and left my office.

"Hi Dad," shouted Colin from across the newsroom as he walked through the maze of reporters' cubicles. All the reporters love Colin. He constantly asks questions about everyone's work, which reporters love, and often comes up with the oddest angles and perspectives on issues, which they also love and frequently use in their leads. His school is not too far away from the newspaper. When school lets out and if his baby-sitter or dad is not there to pick him up, a reporter will walk him over to the newsroom. They actually fight for the chance to do so because it means they get his full attention for one of their stories. Sometimes he stays until his dad finishes work. Other times, his babysitter takes him home and starts dinner for them. They make it work and with just a quick glance at Colin you know he's a happy, secure, curious kid who is completely loved and taken care of.

Colin is one of my kids, too, just like his dad, so we've built up our own relationship. I know he loves science and I do my best to direct him in that area either through websites, news articles for kids, and even books now and then. YouTube has great stuff for kids who love science. I love watching his sense of wonder when he discovers something new about the world. His curiosity seems bottomless. He keeps asking me why and how things work. I love it. I love him.

Lately, we've been talking a lot about his dad. He doesn't know why, and I don't try to explain the why part, but he senses his dad's depression and overall view of the world. He knows something has changed. He remembers his dad not being like that before. He has also told me that he can tell when his dad tries to switch off his feelings when he comes into the room, but he can't flip the switch that quickly. Colin sometimes catches him with anger in his eyes and even tears. This scares him, but he doesn't know what to do to help.

So we talk a lot about his dad and what's going on in his life and this really picked up after I told him about total solar eclipses and that one was going to happen in Idaho in August. When he found that out, he began to plan, on his own, a road trip for he and his dad to see the total solar eclipse in Idaho. He said it might be the miracle that he'd been waiting for.

I don't actually remember using the word *miracle* when Colin and I were talking about solar eclipses, but they are one of those cool things that makes me proud of the guy I work for. Any scientist can logically explain them and they can also tell you that they are not really that rare. In other words, they are not miracles. There's a few of them every year though not all of them are total. Basically, the moon gets in the way of the sun as it is shining down on the earth and this casts a shadow that is around 50 miles wide which sweeps across the land as the earth turns. The land area within the shadow makes that section of the earth completely dark just like in the middle of the night. There is no light at all because it's in the totality zone. It can be hard for people to see one because the earth is mostly water (around three-fourths of this planet is ocean) so the eclipses do not often occur on land and near people. There's no one around to actually see them, but, of course, they still happen.

But you know what's really cool about total solar eclipses? It has to do the with the number 400. When I told Colin about the upcoming eclipse in Idaho in August, I also told him about the 400 thing. Man, you should have seen his eyes light up. The 400 thing helps explain just how rare a total solar eclipse actually is because more than a few things need to line up just so. I think that's where the *miracle* idea started sprouting in his head even though I'm pretty sure I didn't use that word.

So what's the 400 thing?

Have you ever noticed that the sun and a full moon look about the same size on the horizon or even a bit further up in the sky? They are each like a half dollar coin in size, right? Okay, so this is because the sun's diameter is about 400 times larger than the moon's diameter. The sun is also 400 times farther away from the earth than the moon is from the earth. So this 400 times thing works in two ways. The diameter of the sun and moon are 400 times different (of course, the sun is bigger) and the distance between the earth and the moon is 400 times shorter than the distance between the earth and the sun. This means that when everything lines up, meaning when the moon gets in the way of the sun shining on the earth at exactly the right time, a total solar eclipse is possible. It wouldn't be possible if not for the 400 times thing. For example, if the distance between the moon and the earth was 500 times smaller than the distance between the sun and the earth and the diameter of both was still at 400 times, it wouldn't create a total solar eclipse. The same thing goes if the diameter of the sun was 500 times larger than the diameter of the moon but the distance part was still at 400. For both measurements (the diameter and the distance), it has to be spot on 400 to have a total solar eclipse. If the two measurements are different and the moon gets in the way of the sun, there is still an eclipse, but it's not necessarily a total solar eclipse. There will be a sliver of the sun still shining down onto the earth. There can still be quite a bit of light from this small sliver of sun that is revealed around the moon because it doesn't completely block out the sun's rays shining down on the earth. This is because of the size difference either from the diameter or distance. Get it?

Now, here's the cool part. Of course, there are gazillions of stars and planets in the universe and most of the planets have moons. Jupiter alone has something like 79 moons and it's the moons that cast the shadow. But to get a total solar eclipse, which is basically a complete and perfect shadow cast onto a certain point on the planet, the moon and the earth and the sun (i.e. the star that shines light onto a planet) have to be aligned perfectly to cast that shadow *and be of an exact size* in terms of diameter and distance. In the case of our earth, that alignment and size is a factor of 400. So if the universe has a gazillion stars, planets, and moons, how many of them are of a perfect distance and perfect diameter so that a total solar eclipse is even possible?

I ain't saying, but just think about how rare that is. I'd say it's a bit of a miracle.

Colin immediately got how eclipses worked, but he freaked out when he understood the whole 400 times thing. He saw it as something beyond science. It was like some kind of miracle. When I told him that a total solar eclipse was coming up in Idaho in August and that the totality path was only a few hours' drive away from where we lived, he immediately began planning a road trip. He saw it for what it was and what it could be. It was the *miracle* that he had been waiting for to help save his dad.

But when he told his dad about it and said that he wanted them to go, Max said no. He had no desire or intention of going to see anything miraculous. He didn't believe in anything anymore. He most especially didn't believe in miracles.

* * *

In the aviation world, there is a phenomenon that pilots call a death spiral. This when their plane, for a variety of different reasons, pitches nose down towards the ground and then slowly starts spinning. The longer the plane is heading nose down, the faster it goes and the more and faster it spins. It becomes difficult for pilots to arrest the fall and correct the spin even after they have identified the cause of the plane pitching down (for example, a faulty rudder, stuck flaps, wind shear, stalled engine, etc...). The solution is apparent, but the pilot cannot execute it because the drop and the spin, i.e. the death spiral, is so acute that G Forces prevent the pilot from arresting the fall or correcting the spin. It's a fight against gravity and it's really hard to defeat gravity.

Max was in a death spiral. He was getting worse every day. He did nothing but report on how much people hated each other, why they did so, and how quickly and viciously they would push buttons to make others even more angry and more hateful towards each other. It was accurate reporting that someone had to do. It was his job and, professional that he was, he was doing it, but at a huge cost to him personally. Colin was watching it all and he didn't know what to do. It's all we talk about anymore. He's no longer interested in science, YouTube videos, or any of the stories that the reporters are working on. He keeps going back to the miracle that was due to appear in Idaho. He keeps asking me to convince his dad to go. He even said, with tears in his eyes which broke my heart, that I should make him go.

"Tell him to write about it. You're the editor. That's your job, right?" he implored adding that it was a good story and that the 400 thing could become part of the deep background of the story and would make for an interesting lead. He's picked up a lot of journo-speak. I told Colin that I would talk to his dad, but I couldn't really make him go.

A few days later, after Max and I had finished an editorial discussion of news stories and topics for the week, I asked him how things were going at home.

"What do you mean?" he asked.

"Just that. How's it going? Colin seems a bit preoccupied lately."

"Why you asking me? The two of you are always talking together. When I ask him later what you were talking about, he won't tell me. What's up with that?"

"Come on. You know we're close and talk a lot," I said.

"Yeah, but it's not the same, is it? Something's different."

"You're right. Something is different. You're different. He can see that clear as a bell."

"I'm not different."

"No, Max, you are. I know you got a shit deal with the politics desk, but you're the best reporter on this newspaper. I can't move you to another desk because no one can cover these issues as well as you. These things have to be written about. You know that. Come on, man. What's going on?"

There was a long pause. Complete silence. Max just sat in his chair, staring out the window, looking at nothing. He started to say something, but then his jaw tightened up. I could feel the stress and pain coming out from him, traveling across my desk, and hitting me. I mean, I could really feel it.

"He wants to see the eclipse," he said softly as tears rolled down his cheeks.

"Yeah, I know. He even asked me to assign it to you as a story."

"He says it's a miracle. Something about 400 times something. I'm not sure what the hell he's talking about."

"Maybe you should ask," I replied.

There was a long silence. I looked at him while he looked out the window. Finally, Max slowly stood up, sighed deeply while still staring at seemingly nothing out the window, and murmured something about getting back to work. He didn't look at me. He just kept looking out the window. It was like I wasn't even there. He turned, nodded in my direction, and slowly walked out of my office. He walked to his desk and slumped down in his chair. I don't think he moved for more than an hour. He just sat there. Staring at nothing.

When I arrived to work early the next morning, Max was already at his desk. This was unusual since he generally sticks around at home after taking Colin to school. After that, he returns home to read the news online, drink coffee, and make some work-related phone calls from home. I allow the reporters to work from wherever they want as long as they get their pieces in. None of them arrive to the newsroom before I do. They start filtering in around 10. But that day Max was already at his desk when I got in before 8 AM. He was sitting up straight and leaning into his computer reading something online.

"Whoa! You're in early," I said. "Is everything okay?"

"Yeah, yeah, it's fine, but I need to talk to you. Give me a second."

Half an hour later, he came into my office and told me what happened the night before.

"We had a big fight," Max said as he started to tear up again.

Colin tried again to convince his dad that they needed to go to Idaho to see the solar eclipse. The fight started over whether or not the eclipse was science or a miracle. Max refused to acknowledge it as a miracle and kept trying to tell Colin that it was a simple scientific event. It happened all the time. Colin responded by saying that science and miracles can be the same thing.

"Why can't they? Why can't they? He said that over and over to me," Max said replaying the conversation. "He kept going on and on about the 400 times thing. I get it now. That's what I was reading about when you came in. But that's not a miracle. That's also science. I am not going to raise my kid believing in bullshit miracles that can be easily explained by a scientist. He wants to fucking believe in God. What the hell is that all about? In today's world, there's supposed to be a God? How can there be a God with what's happening in this country?"

"Why can't they be both?" I asked.

"Fuck you!" Max shouted.

He immediately seemed to regret it. There was a long pause. Another complete silence.

"I mean...sorry but he's my son. I know you guys are close and have your own friendship and believe me I'm very, very thankful for that. But this is too much. There are no miracles in this world. Not now. Not after 2016. The real miracle would be his mom coming back, but she ain't coming back. And I told him that, but he doesn't remember her. He was too small when she left."

"He's never mentioned her to me," I said.

Another long pause. Total silence again.

"He said he couldn't remember her, but that it was okay. He said it was okay because he has everything he needs. He has me. He said I'm the last face he sees at night and I'm the first face he sees in the morning. I told him it's because I put him to bed every night and then I wake him up every morning. But he said he feels like I never leave him. Ever. Like I am standing above him and looking down at him all night long to be sure he's okay while he's sleeping. The entire time. He's worried I'm not going to be there anymore because of all the shit that's happening with this fucking job."

The tears are pouring down his face now, but I can tell they are not only sad tears. They are a mix of happy and sad tears pouring up and out from his heart. I've never had a kid so I don't know from personal experience, but I imagine hearing your own child tell you how crucial you are in life must have a tremendous impact. A big responsibility too.

"Anyway, we're gonna go," he said. "I guess I have to."

* * *

I decided to go as well. Well, actually, I was told to go, but I wasn't supposed to tell Max or Colin that I would be there. I was being sent to be sure that everything went okay, but I had to go secretly. They needed to make their journey on their own and see it all for themselves. To be honest, I wanted to go. In all my assignments, I had never seen a total solar eclipse. I was as excited as Colin about seeing the whole thing.

Colin learned about a place called Hailey Hot Springs which was completely within the totality zone. There were hot springs there, as the name implies, but also regular swimming pools, cottages, a pizza restaurant, a campground, and a golf course. It was basically a small, local getaway for people who lived nearby. But for that brief moment of time, it was one of the best places in America to see the total solar eclipse because it was going to be a completely cloud free day.

There were a lot of people there. The sky was clear blue with not a cloud in sight. The eclipse was scheduled for totality at 10:47 AM and it was supposed to last about three minutes. At 10:30 AM, pretty much everyone was wearing those special glasses so you could look directly at the sun without hurting your eyes. I did, too, and it was cool to watch the moon slowly move across the sun, one small slice at a time, blocking out completely any bit of light. By 10:30, more than half the sun was covered, but the sun still seemed to be shining as brightly and as warmly as any other blue sky day in August. Guess it shows you just how strong the sun actually is.

I mixed in with a large group of people in order to see the eclipse and also not be noticed by Max or Colin. Looking out from that group, I noticed something interesting. It was two people, a 40-something year old man and a young girl who looked to be around 12 years old. The girl was wearing a quite pretty dress with a bow in her hair as if she was attending a piano recital or going to church. The man was also nicely dressed up. They were standing apart from the groups, quite close to each other, and they were looking up. They were wearing the special glasses and were fixated on looking directly at the sun. They somehow looked different. Maybe it was their body posture or how they didn't seem to move at all. They were like statues, standing side by side, with their heads angled up towards the sun as if they were waiting for something to arrive. I noticed the man had one of his hands on the girl's shoulder. I assumed they were father-daughter, or at least they definitely looked as such. They somehow stood out among the growing crowd of people who were also looking up at the sun.

Max, being the consummate journalist that he is, also noticed them and actually went up to them to chat. He broke up the reverie of the man who turned to speak with Max briefly, but the girl continued to look up. She didn't move at all. It was like she was waiting for something to come pouring out from the sun. From what I could tell, the man quickly explained something to Max and then went back to looking up at the sun. Max nodded and slowly walked away, looking back at them one more time before leaving to find out where Colin had gone.

Colin was all over the place and beyond giddy. He kept up a running commentary for anyone and everyone within earshot to hear. He accurately explained the 400 times thing to a fairly large group of adults and kids who seemed to congregate around him listening intently. He held court not like an 8-year old boy from Montana, but more like Neil deGrasse Tyson giving a lecture about the cosmos at an international symposium. It was fun to watch. Neither Colin or Max noticed me.

At around 10:40, it began to get noticeably cooler, but only slightly darker, kind of like dusk. Remember it was a beautiful blue sky August day. The cooler part struck me as kind of weird and the others in my group were also talking about it. I'm guessing the temperature dropped at least 10 degrees in just a couple minutes. It was kinda like walking into an air-conditioned movie theater from the outside on a hot day.

Looking through the glasses, the moon's shadow kept creeping across the sun until there was just a sliver of sun still visible. The rest of the space, where the sun used to be, was as round as a basketball and completely black. It was easy to see where the sun used to shine, but had now been blocked by the moon. It was also easy to see how a total solar eclipse works because the diameter of the moon really did exactly cover the diameter of the sun. The 400 times thing was easier to understand because we could finally see it. If it were off even a little bit in terms of diameter and I guess distance, there would still be a sliver of sun visible to shed light on the earth. It wouldn't be total. The idea that the 400 times thing was a miracle, and not just science, began to make sense.

When there was just a slight sliver of sun left, it became darker and darker. I don't know for sure if it became colder, but it felt colder but also calmer, like a perfect summer evening. The tiniest slice of sun was still visible, but there was a buzz among the group because everyone knew that totality and then the corona was coming. Everyone was wearing the glasses and staring directly up at the sun. The moon kept moving across the sun. It was going to block out completely that last slice of light.

It was coming. Totality was close.

And then just like that, the corona appeared, a dark black hole emerged in the sky, and everyone there, me included, *just plain knew* there was something behind that hole.

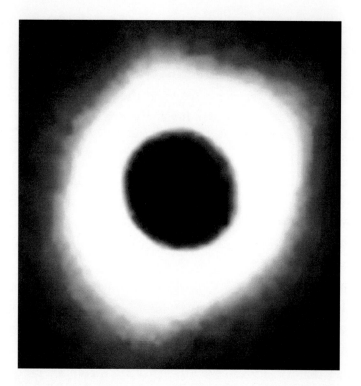

The dark black hole, where the sun used to be, was much, much blacker than the rest of the sky. It seemed to be sucking in everything in the same way that it had sucked out any shred of sunlight that had been shining down onto the earth. It felt like, if you were tall enough, that you could reach your hand through the hole and something or someone would grasp your hand on the other side. And it would be a warm hand. It would feel good as if the hole was a portal or a door to something tremendously beautiful. The warm hand was inviting you in and ready to pull you up and through the portal. At that time, at that moment, everyone in my small little group *knew* we were not alone. There was something behind that hole that a scientist could never explain.

Many people started crying. Some were hugging each other, laughing, and began dancing around. An older couple began to dance the waltz around the group, sloppily kissing each other, laughing, and trying to look up all at the same time. Others were like statues, transfixed on the corona and the dark black hole that had suddenly appeared in the sky. They couldn't stop staring at it.

I looked over at Max and Colin and also at the father and daughter.

"Daddy, there's a hole in the sky!" screamed Colin. "Lookit, lookit, there's a hole in the sky."

Colin briefly looked away from the eclipse and towards his dad who was transfixed, stuck in place like a statue, and staring up with his mouth wide open. Colin ran to him and plowed his entire face into his dad's stomach and wrapped his arms around his waist. I could see how tightly his skinny arms were wrapped around his dad and squeezing him. Then, he let go and started to run and dance in circles around his dad, looking up, laughing, doing cartwheels, and shouting to everyone that there was a hole in the sky.

The father and daughter seemed to step forward as if they wanted to walk into the hole. It looked like the father was talking to someone and his daughter held her hands up like a toddler asking to be picked up. They didn't seem to notice anything around them or any of the people who were laughing, dancing, crying, and shouting. They just kept looking up, never taking their eyes off the hole in the sky.

Max had dropped to his knees while still staring up. Like the father daughter duo, he seemed oblivious to the chaos around him including his own son laughing, shouting, and doing cartwheels around him. He just kept staring up. He looked like a statue.

The totality lasted about three minutes and then it slowly became lighter and lighter. Then, almost as suddenly as it had become dark, it was once again a sunny blue sky day in August. Everyone kept looking up, but eventually there was no reason to. The moon kept traveling across the face of the sun, but it was seemingly no longer important to watch that happen. Instead, everyone looked at each other in silence. Some were still crying. Others were hugging and kissing. Many had all the color drained from their faces and many also had their mouths still hanging wide open.

The older couple who had been doing the waltz had fallen to the ground, holding hands, and with their heads next to each other. They were trying to control not their laughter, but massive giggling fits as they kept turning their heads to kiss each other. Suddenly, the man picked his head up and quickly looked around. He then rolled over on top of the woman and whispered something in her ear causing her to shout out while trying to push him off. Her face was already red as a baboon's butt, but it somehow turned even redder when his hand reached up under her shirt causing them both to somehow giggle even more.

Max was still on his knees, but he was no longer looking up nor looking at anything in particular. He just stared straight forward with a peaceful look on his face. This didn't change even after Colin jumped onto his back shouting and hugging him from behind while still shouting about the hole that was in the sky.

The father and daughter had turned towards each other and into a deep embrace. The girl was sobbing while the father held her head against his chest and gently stroked her hair. He whispered something into her ear and the girl nodded but continued to sob.

Suddenly, I heard Colin shout, "Peter! Daddy, Peter's here."

Colin had spotted me in the group and sprinted the 25 or so yards separating us. When he was about five feet away, he leapt into the air with his arms straight out and flying like he was Superman. I caught him just as his head hit my chest. He wrapped his arms and legs around me and turned his head up and, for the very first time, kissed me. Once on the neck and once on the cheek. He whispered into my ear, "Thank you. Oh, thank you so much."

He wiggled down and shouted to Max, "Daddy, Peter's here." He grabbed my hand and pulled me over to where Max was kneeling down and still staring straight ahead.

Max looked up at me and didn't seem at all surprised to see me. It was like he knew I was going to be there.

"I didn't know what to expect, but I wasn't expecting that," he said.

"What do you mean?"

"I saw... I'm not sure what I saw, but I didn't think it existed. I was sure it didn't."

"What did you see?"

"What about you? What did you see?" he asked.

"You go first. In fact, give me 700 words on what you saw and we'll run it."

"Maybe it should be 400 words," Max said causing both of us to laugh.

"Up to you."

"Hey, you guys," shouted Colin. "Let's go swimming!"

"Good idea," Max said as he got up off his knees. He looked over at the father and daughter. "You guys go ahead. I'll meet you there. I want to talk to some people first."

"Okay. It's a deal," said Colin. "Come on, Peter. Let's go."

Colin grabbed my hand and started pulling me away from everyone and towards the hot springs and swimming pool area. "They got slides, a diving board, and everything here. Even a game room. It's cool! We can have pizza later. Come on. Iddle be fun."

And of course, it was fun. We spent the rest of the day at the pool with trips to dip into the hot springs pool as well. There was a ping pong table in the game room and we played a few games. We ordered pizza and ate it poolside. I taught Colin how to dive from the diving board without belly flopping and he taught me the cannonball.

As for Max, he was an entirely different person that entire day. Really for the following weeks as well, and honestly way beyond that. He was happy and thankful that he had such a great kid. Of course, his journo job was still a job that he had to do and the hate never ceased nor his need to report on it, but he no longer let it hit him the way it had. He realized that he was no longer alone and in fact he never had been.

Max wrote his op-ed about the solar eclipse. It created a flood of letters to the editor, the most ever I was told, and pretty much every letter was positive and thankful. My favorite was from an older woman who had been diagnosed with pancreatic cancer. It was already at stage four and she really had just a handful of months left to live. She had kids and her kids had kids and some of those kids had also begun to have kids. It was a salty letter with colorful references to a "*shit ton of grandkids*" and "*that bitch cancer*" which would ultimately prevent her from seeing her grandkids and great grandkids get married and start their own families. She wanted to be there for that. She wrote that she hoped to be a great, great grandma, but probably wouldn't be and that had made her angry. However, she also wrote that she had gained an appreciation for what she did have and was thankful for her life.

"Being angry is such a waste of time. It does nothing but prolong the hate. How many people get to be great greats? How about even just a great grandma? Shit! Even a regular grandma. I was all that and more. How can I possibly be angry when I've been lucky enough to have such a large family and now (after reading Max's piece) I have some evidence that we are not alone and that everything is, in the end, going to be okay. We'll be okay. That works for me. Thanks, Max. You made this old lady ready for her next adventure."

So, I'm going to finish my story by letting Max tell his. I didn't edit a word nor did I suggest the title. This is all Max.

Memo From the Landlord

By Max S with a life-saving contribution from Colin S

"I am the master of my fate. I am the captain of my soul."

Nearly 150 years ago, William Ernest Henley penned his epic poem **Invictus**. These words, especially the last two lines quoted above, have kept me going for most of my life in particular during the darkest of times. However, it was only yesterday that I realized Henley's poem was missing one sentence, just one line of words. He didn't tell the whole story. Maybe he didn't know the whole story. But I know the whole story now. An 8-year-old Montana boy taught me the full story, and by doing so he saved my life.

Along with so many Montanans, my son Colin and I journeyed south to Idaho to witness the total solar eclipse. Colin wanted to see a miracle that he was convinced would occur. I didn't believe him nor did I believe in miracles. Quite honestly, I didn't believe in much of anything anymore. Henley's poetic words no longer carried me. I reluctantly agreed to go with some vague hope to see science in action and possibly re-gain a sense of peace, redemption, and belief in a world that I felt had been destroyed. We both got what we were seeking.

It came from a black hole in the sky. The scientific explanation for this black hole in the sky is compelling and logical. It's even quite beautiful. Some might say it's miraculous. But, just like the last two lines of **Invictus**, the full story is not told. There's more, a lot more.

The black hole in the sky appeared when the totality of the solar eclipse arrived. This meant the moon had completely blocked out the sun and the only thing remaining, and only for about three minutes, was a deep, dark, and very black hole in the sky. Everyone who was there saw that. I think everyone also saw something, or maybe someone, else behind the hole.

I interviewed an older couple who must have been in their 70s and asked them what they saw. They were potato farmers from that part of Idaho. They looked and talked like the most salt-of-the-earth rural farmer types you would ever meet so it was surprising what they said amid their massive giggling fits and red faces. The wife kept punching her husband in the ribs, laughing, and telling him to "*shut your pie hole.*"

The old man told me that he didn't know what he saw, but that whatever it was it made him hot and ready to do his wife right there on the grass, in the park, and to hell with everyone around them. If they wanted to watch, so be it. His wife was game, too, but they couldn't get started because they were both laughing too hard.

Before the eclipse occurred, I spoke to a man who was there with his daughter. Maybe it was their clothes or something else, but they somehow stood out among the crowd of people waiting for totality to arrive. I learned that they had lost their wife/mother just a few months before to cancer and were still very much in mourning. They didn't understand why, but they were pulled to Hailey Hot Springs to see the eclipse and hopefully gain some sense of peace. They did.

"She was there," the man told me with tears in his eyes. "She was there on the other side of that hole. She told us to not worry about her anymore and that everything was going to be okay. She missed us but she was okay and we should be okay, too. Everything was good. She's in a good place. She told us she was okay and that we have to be okay, too." His daughter said nothing, but kept hugging her dad with her eyes closed and tears streaming down her face.

As for me, it was not a what, but a who. I don't know who the who was or how to call him/her/it so I am just going to say that I met The Landlord. Since I'm a journalist, I had to do an interview. I had a scoop, but I totally bitched it up by asking all the wrong questions.

I thought I had it nailed. For the past several months, I've done nothing but report on the culture wars of America so I had all the questions ready. I started with the science/atheist/agnostic arguments about proof of existence, evilness in the world, and how religion is manipulated by leaders for their personal gain. I got nothing back. I switched to the greatest hits arguments of the evangelicals about God's moral order, salvation, and such and even more eye rolling was the result. It was frustrating. I had the interview of my life but I was completely missing the point by asking all the wrong questions. Exasperated, I told The Landlord that I never believed he/she/it existed and based on my interview I was apparently right. In response, I got the one quotable quote for my story.

"That's okay. I have always believed in you and I always will. You have never been alone in this world and you never will be."

I blew the interview, but I got a bit of an answer though I'm not too sure to which question I had asked. Mostly, though, I found out what the missing words were for the final line of Henley's poem.

I am the master of my fate.

I am the captain of my soul.

And I am not alone on my journey.

I learned more. I learned that in the entire universe, with all its stars, planets, and moons that exist within, the chances of getting everything lined up for a perfect solar eclipse is very rare. It really is a miracle. But even more miraculous is that an eight-year old Montana boy knew this, and he also knew that love conquers all. All the black holes in the sky in all the skies of the universe can never equal the profound power of a little boy who is trying to save his dad's life.

The End

Sam Korsmoe

Sam Korsmoe is an American writer who has been living and working in Vietnam for nearly 20 years. He is the founder of the **Saigon Writers Club**, has published two books, and is awaiting publication of a third book that he co-authored about the future of Vietnam.

This is a true story...... Well not exactly, but at least it's based on a true story. I created a narrator and let him tell the story with some creative embellishments to push the story along. However, it's true that there was a total solar eclipse near my Montana home in 2017. It's true that the time period in America back then was quite ugly. It's true that my son and I (the kid in the middle in the photo above) travelled to see the eclipse. It's true that a dark black hole suddenly appeared in the sky. It's true that I saw, felt, touched, and/or connected with something or someone behind that hole in the sky. And to this day, I am so very thankful that I made that connection. It gave me a sense of hope that I thought had been lost.

CHAPTER 5

More Than Enough

By

Garrett MacLean

More.

That was the answer to all of life's problems. More. Do more. Get more. See more. Be more.

Enough? Pshh! There is no such thing as "enough."

Enough was the worst word to add to your lexicon. It didn't mean the end was near. It meant the end had passed you up a long time ago. It didn't mean you were finished. It meant YOU had been finished with already.

Enough? Ha! No. More. More is the answer. More is the only..........

"Care to add your two cents, Tom? Tom?"

My reflection in the northwest mirror of the corner office gained resolution. I had been daydreaming again. Daydreaming about More. More money. More sex. More time. More.....

"Tom, we were just going over the projections for next quarter and wanted to hear your input," Bill said standing at the front of the room with a PowerPoint presentation behind him. It was the one that I made yesterday and agreed to let him use.

"Mo... these look good Bill. Keep going," I said putting to ease my restless right leg syndrome and swivelling back to face the front of the room where a tunnel of black and blue suits and way too expensive hair-cuts led to Bill's shiny forehead standing in as the light at the end of the tunnel. There he stood, glimmering in his white oxford shirt.

He seemed so far away, further than usual.

Bill was so sure of himself, I thought. I was sure his collared shirt needed more starch though. I could see the wrinkles in his collar from the opposite end of the tunnel. I guess he wasn't that far away. Bill never cared that much about his shirt though whether it was a little too small or that his shoulders were a little too big. He stayed calm, cool, collected, always, ever since I had met him freshman year back at Wharton.

If he did have a guilty conscience, I never picked up on it.

I wonder if he ever noticed my guilty conscience. If he has, he's never pointed it out. He very well knew I was cheating on my wife and her on me and never brought it up once since it slipped off my tongue a few months back after way too many Jack n' cokes flying back from another business trip to Taipei.

"Alright, everyone good meeting today. Get back on the phones and we'll talk at the end of the week," I could hear Bill echoing inside his chamber at the other end of the tunnel as I was staring out the window one more time thinking about....

"Tom, Tommy, buddy, what's up man? I can smell the Jack on you again and if you haven't really noticed nobody was sitting next to you, again. What's going on? Were you out with Sydney because..."

My reflection gains resolution in the window once again and I swivel in my chair towards Bill. I look him in the eye and hold contact as if to remind him of the conversation we already had without having to spark up an unnecessary sequel.

Bill continued, "Sorry, bud. It's just ...you're not looking good. Where were you last night? You didn't answer any of my calls. Don't tell me you were doing it again."

"What? I can't stalk my own wife? She stalks me! She's a lawyer for Christ's sake. There's no arguing with her. This time it felt different. I think she's moved on to someone else. Something's off. She's coming home at different times, breaking the pattern. She knows I know." I check my watch, 3:17. My clock is always five minutes fast ever since I missed a track meet back in high school because I was five minutes late and missed the team bus. Never again I told myself. I look at the clock hanging on the wall. It's exactly 3:12 as I expected.

"Look, I'm worried about you Tom. You're not acting right," Bill starts up.

"Not acting right? Ha! Besides, we're men. We don't worry about each other. We deal with our own shit. Besides, like I'm the only one ordering bottle service when we go to Taipei."

"I'm not talking about that. I'm talking about Lehigh Import, Tom. The board met last night."

"What do you mean the board met last night? Without me? Why didn't you call me?

"I did call you. 14 times. Why didn't you answer? Where were you?" Bill repeated.

"Doesn't matter. What did the board talk about that was so important? I asked.

"You're out Tom."

"What did you just say to me?"

"There was a vote and the board ruled that you weren't fit to run this company anymore."

"Not fit to run this company anymore? It's my fucking name on the door, Bill. Well, my father's name. Besides, you can't throw me out. I'm the one who got you a job here in the first place. Remember the summer after school?"

"I know you did and I want you to know I had nothing to do with this."

"Then, why are you the one telling me? Why not what's his face?" I swallow a hiccup wreaking of mostly Jack and not much Coke.

"I've known you the longest and so I thought it made sense that you should hear it from me."

"You thought it made sense? As if the world still makes sense," I said swivelling back away from Bill while my restless right leg kicked back into gear.

"Look I gotta go, the board will contact you soon about selling off your shares. Go get something to eat or better yet get some rest, Tom. You look like shit."

"Always great seeing you too Billy Boy. By the way, you're welcome for the PowerPoint."

Bill closes the door behind him without a word and walked away down the hall and into the elevator.

"Out?" I hiccup again, looking back out the northwest window again losing resolution. "Out of his fucking mind."

***

After daydreaming a bit more about More, I stand up, grab my briefcase, check my watch and then check my phone. Why hasn't she answered my calls? I wonder if she's still upset. 14 missed outbound calls to Sydney. I scroll down a bit further on my call history, yep, Bill was right: 14 missed inbound calls in a matter of an hour. I walk out to my car, pile in, hiccup once more, the Jack was losing its residue, and head on home.

Nowhere else to go but home if Syd's not answering.

I pull out of the parking lot. Out? How can I be out? The hell with it. I don't want to work there anymore anyways. I want something else. I want something more... for myself.

I pull into the driveway and notice Sam's car is still there. That's weird. It's Friday. Normally she would be where I think she would be. I walk inside. Something's off. I can feel it cause I've felt it for a long time.

"Sam?" I call out. "Sammy, you home?"

I drop my keys on the counter. Someone's upstairs.

I walk up the stairs slowly. There are people up there. Fuck, what if it's Sydney confessing to Sam? She has threatened me before. Wait, no. It's Sam. I recognize her voice and the other voice I recognize too. No. Not in my house. It's one thing to cheat on your husband in a cheap hotel on a weekend, but in my house on a Friday. I'm gonna kill that douchebag attorney, Edward Steel.

I kick open the door, "Who the fuck do you think you are coming into my house Edwar...." I stop mid-sentence.

Me and Sam's bedroom was custom designed by this fancy interior designer that Sam's lawyer friend, Edward Steel, swore by. Sam called him Eddie. Every single piece of furniture was hand-picked by this short Italian guy who was born in Florence. Supposedly, his whole family has been interior designers dating all the way back to when the House of Medici bankrolled their family. I wonder if Lorenzo de Medici would have ever envisioned my wife of fifteen years bent over our $3,000 suede ottoman with my best friend of 20 years right behind her with his wrinkly oxford shirt unbuttoned and his black trousers unzipped and barely hanging on to his hips.

"Oh shit! Oh shit!" Sam and Bill say in unison, trying to return their clothes to the appropriate spots.

I say nothing. I've seen enough. I make a 180, walk back down the stairs, retracing my steps, grab my car keys, and head to the garage in one swift motion. I turn on the car and sit in the garage for a second with the garage door shut.

I knew she'd been cheating. I just didn't know with who. And I knew Bill had been running around because he'd always been running around. For someone who was so sure of himself, his last three wives were pretty damn sure they didn't want anything to do with him. Three wives in five years. If there was a sport for failed marriages, he would be the 1998 Michael Jordan of divorce, the face of a three-peat train wreck dynasty.

It was getting stuffy, harder to breathe. I was feeling a headache coming on. Why not just sit here for the afternoon? The sound of the engine is soothing. What else is there to lose?

I could hear someone coming from the kitchen. It's Sam. I recognize her footsteps. I recognize Bill's in the distance too.

Isn't it weird that we can remember the sound of how someone walks, but we don't remember when we first remembered it?

Before she comes to the side door of the garage, I open the main garage door and reverse out. What else is there to lose? I ask myself again.

Just then I hear a loud thump.

What the...?

"Wiggles! Nooooo," Sam screams as she comes running out of the garage and onto the driveway. I sat there for a second in the driver's seat. It was me facing the road ahead, the sun was getting really low, subtly peeking over the horizon. Sam was holding our dog in her arms, Wiggles, who was doing anything but. And then there was Bill poking his head out the side garage door. His pants were back on, but his fly was still down. Nice, Bill. I shake my head, face the road again, push my foot down on the accelerator, and head towards the light.

Talk about the goldest of all the golden hours.

***

"Evening sir, what can I do you for?" said the hotel receptionist.

"I need a room," I say.

"We have one last suite available. Double queen. Smoking Room. How's that sound?"

"That sounds fine." I don't smoke, but I'm too tired to ask for something else.

The receptionist hands me the key for my room, I mozie on over to the elevator, hit 7, lean back against the back of the elevator, and look at my reflection in the ceiling. "I need a vacation," I say to myself.

"Me too," an older gentleman responds back to me.

I didn't realize I was speaking out loud or that there was someone else in the elevator with me.

"I always wanted to travel around the world," he continues on, "you know, like Anthony Bourdain style or something like that. Check out Southeast Asia, that sort of thing."

He was nice. I was tired.

"Yeah," I said.

The bell goes off. Floor 7. I give the old man one of those half-crescent moon smiles that you practice 50 times a day in the corporate world. I had crafted mine to perfection. What looks like dimples were craters carved out of quarterly board meetings.

I walk down the hallway and find my room, C737. I press the key to the door, it unlocks. The room is empty and cold and grey. I put my briefcase down and pass out face down on the bed.

Job. Wife. Friend. No, best friend. Best friend AND business partner. Dog. Life. All gone. In one big fuck-you-and-everything-that's-yours-swoop.

I've officially been inducted into the Hall of Fame of Getting Fucked Over.

God, I'm too hungover for this. The grey room begins to fade to black.

I wake up at exactly 5:55. I check the clock on the nightstand: 6:00. I can't tell if I fell asleep for ten minutes or ten hours or ten years. Judging by the color outside, I'm guessing it is now morning.

"Syd, I know we said," I began to roll over, "no more room service because of what happened last time, but..." I look around. Syd's not there and it hits me like a bag of bricks exploding out of my eye sockets. Oh yeah. I sigh and remember why I'm lying on a bed inside four grey cigarette-soaked walls.

I had it all, but I wanted more. I always wanted more and look where that's gotten me. I look around and shut my eyes not wanting to face reality.

I stayed holed up in that hotel room for three days. My phone died and I didn't bother to plug it back in. I also hadn't eaten much besides a few mint candies that I had in my pockets so I decided to

call in some room service. A ham sandwich, fries, and a coke. As I'm
waiting, I flip on the TV and wouldn't you have guessed it—Anthony
Bourdain is on.

"...Going to Vietnam the first time was life-changing for sure; maybe
because it was all so new and different to my life before and the world I
grew up in. The food, culture, landscape and smell; they're all inseparable.
It just seemed like another planet; a delicious one that sort of sucked me in
and never let go..."

I thought of the old man from the other day in the elevator. It wasn't
the wrinkles that covered the top of his hands or his temples that made
him appear elderly. It was his soul or I should say the lack thereof. That
old man probably never took a vacation in his life.

I remember then what the old man said. "I always wanted to travel
around the world, you know like Anthony Bourdain style or something
like that. Check out Southeast Asia, that sort of thing."

Hell, that's what I'm gonna do, old man, talking as if the old man
was standing there in front of me. I'm gonna get the hell out of dodge.
I can't sit here in this hotel for the rest of my life and live and die off red
and white minted candies. I'm going to Vietnam and that's that.

At that moment, there was a knock at the door. Could it be Syd?
Could be it Sam? Could it be Bill? Could it be the Grim Reaper coming
to room C737 to finish me off? Could it be Wiggles rising from the
dead ready to seek vengeance on me?

I stand up too fast. The room goes from grey to fuzzy black like
static on the tv. I realized I hadn't stood up in a while. I stumble over
to the door and look into the eye hole. Of course, it's broken. Classic.
I keep the chain lock hooked and open the door a whole three inches.
It's a slender man with slick hair and slim fingered hands at his side.

The guy looked like the Grim Reaper if the Grim Reaper ever took off its cloak.

"Room service, sir."

"Oh yeah. Uhh, just leave it there and bill it to my room. Thanks."

"Very well," the man replies.

In a matter of minutes, I eat the ham sandwich in six bites and eat the fries six at a time. I drink the soda in six gulps, pull my laptop out, and book my flight. Thank God for airline points.

John F. Kennedy to LAX to Incheon to Tan Son Nhat. And away we go.....

**

I step out of the airport and am greeted by a crop of waving arms asking me to take their taxi to wherever I wanted. I've done this a thousand times before when flying with Bill. Screw Bill.

Seoul. Tokyo. Bangkok. Taipei. Singapore. Beijing. Now, Ho Chi Minh City once again. Good thing I had a taxi already waiting. I keep my head down and fist tight around my suitcase and I walk through the tunnel of people outside of Tan Son Nhat.

I can feel sweat trickling down my back already and my palms were already moist. It was hot and the heat stuck to me and didn't want to let go of its warm embrace.

It felt weird not having a pre-scheduled business meeting to attend or having a restaurant that Bill picked out to go to. What's even weirder is that Syd still hasn't gotten back to me. 18 *more* missed calls from the Incheon terminal. All straight to voicemail.

I've felt alone before. But, with no meeting, no Syd, no Sam, and no Bill, I discovered a new layer of loneliness. Maybe Bourdain was talking about the heat and not the food when he said Vietnam sucked him in. Jesus Christ.

I wore my normal suit despite everything. Dad always said, "Wear a suit when you fly, always. Let people know you mean business, always."

My dad always meant what he said, except when he didn't like when he lied to me about going on a back-to-back business trip to see his mistress whose name I never learned and never wanted to learn.

I pile into the taxi, throw my suitcase onto the other seat, cock my neck to the side, and undo the top button of my white, already soaking, oxford dress shirt. The windows were quickly fogging up before the driver began blasting the AC.

"Aghh... what a day huh?" I grumble, eyes closed facing the roof of the car. For a second, I dozed off, a bit lightheaded from the three double Jack n' Cokes I slammed in Seoul. "What. A. Day." I repeated, pausing between each word with my eyes remaining closed.

The driver said nothing but shot a quick cursory glass into the rear-view mirror and then into the side mirror and we were off to another hotel in a part of the city called Phu Nhuan. On a normal trip, I would stay at the Sheraton as usual. But this was not a usual stay nor a normal trip. It was time for something more different.

It had been a few years since being in Vietnam. Last time, Bill and I only stopped by Ho Chi Minh City and didn't even leave the terminal. We instead got drunk with the stewardesses from our flight at the airline's lobby. Bill got lucky. I didn't. Talk about foreshadowing this shit storm.

Thus, it was my first time *seeing* Ho Chi Minh City up close and not looking from the window seat as we descended into the city. The city felt alive. Nonstop movement everywhere you looked. I look to my left, there are chickens in cages on the back of a motorbike. I look to my right, there is what looks like an entire family on a back of a bike - grandmother, mother, and daughter, back to front. Only the mother sandwiched between the two had a helmet on for some reason. There are people sitting on the side of the road on little red stools like the one Bourdain was sitting on in his show. There are men in suits, women in long dresses, men in construction wear, women in short dresses, all sitting at stainless steel tables with bowls in front of them and chopsticks and spoons in their right and left hands.

We turn the corner and more people sideline the narrow, serpentine street. Boys and girls are walking in the opposite direction of traffic, girls dressed in all white dresses — those must be what they call the "ao dai", boys dressed in white short-sleeved dress shirts and blue pants. They must have just got done with school, I presumed.

The driver pulls up to what looks like a cafe and puts the car in park and nods as if this is the place. He gets out of the car, walks around, and opens my door. I had grown accustomed to cool air within the taxi when the heat of the city came up quick and sucker-punched me. The faucet of sweat that ran down my back turned back on. I scanned upwards looking for an address: 737 Thuong Nguyen Hien. This must be the place.

I shuffle over to the entrance of the cafe and I see an elderly couple sitting down having what looks like coffee together except it's slowly dripping onto a bed of ice. This must be the "phin coffee" I heard about. Damn, they look so content together, I thought. Enjoying a cup of coffee on a Monday afternoon without a care in the world. They looked old, but not weathered, like they had lived plenty of years but still had enough in the tank for plenty more.

The old man stands up, grabs a menu, and motions me towards one of the open seats at the café. I wonder if this is the couple's place: Cafe 737. What an odd name for a place.

***

"You want coffee?" the old man asked.

It was the first thing I heard anyone say to me besides "Taxi! Taxi!" since I arrived and I was shocked to hear English.

"You speak English?" I replied.

"Of course, I speak English. You speak Vietnamese?"

"Sorry, no, I don't speak Vietnamese," I said feeling embarrassed of being THAT American guy who only knows English fulfilling the classic stereotype for all Americans.

"Coffee sounds good, thank you," I continue, "I'm Tom. What's your name?"

"My name Bao. My wife name An" quickly turning his shoulders to the woman still sitting at the other table and still content as anyone could ever be in this weird world we all live in.

"Nice to meet you both," I say smiling.

"Em oi, mot cafe da," Bao yells out to the cafe counter.

In a flash, a young girl, probably mid-twenties, maybe younger, appears with a silver tray in her hands. She stops and places a small glass of what looks like tea on the table. I can see the small flakes floating around in the glass. Then, she places a glass cup with ice and a silver coffee phin, same as the one Bao and An had, in front of me. Darkness slowly drips from the phin onto the ice, ever gently melting the ice cube altering their density like a canyon eroding over a millennia. The girl does a slight bow, barely perceptible, her hair falls over her face. I didn't get a good look at her, but something told me there was a beautiful face underneath and that most likely I'll have to order another coffee to get a better look.

"Thank you," I say as she turns around.

"First time in Vietnam?" Bao says. I didn't realize he was still there. It was like the girl and Bao were on stage but the spotlight was on the girl now and Bao was the supporting actor stuck in the shadows.

"What? Uhh, yeah. I mean, no. Not ....well kinda. What's her name?" I said slowly lifting my chin up motioning to the girl walking away.

"Her name Chi."

"Chi. Okay," I repeated the name, trying to store it somewhere in my mind so that I wouldn't forget it. Thank God it was a short name too. Longer names I never remembered for some reason.

A few other people walked into the cafe. Bao smiled, did a slight bow, and attended to the new customers. I was left alone at my table.

I looked out at the road, more students were walking by. Bikes whizzed by too and fro. Small blue trucks with bricks or trash drove by. A woman pedaled along the street with a huge crate attached to her bike and what sounded like a recording was playing, *"Bap Xao De, bap xao de,"*

What on earth could that mean?

***

I look back at the darkness dripping into the glass cup. The yin slowly consuming the yang.

Motorbikes continue to whiz by.

"Bap Xao De."

Drip. Drip. Drip.

Vroom. Vroom.

Bap Xao De.

Drip. Drip.

Vroom.

Bap Xao....

I fell further and further into my seat and deeper into a state of relaxation, almost stuck in a sunken place. It felt like I was the smoke being vacuumed back into a Genie's bottle.

All around me, everything continued into nothingness. Shapes blurred and became formless.

Noise deafened. Colors muted. Drip. Vroom. *Bap. Xao. De.....*

"Do you want some more coffee?"

I snap out of it and look up in the direction the noise came from.

It's Bao. He's standing over me. He looks older. A little more weath-ered, almost looking like he's running on empty now. The girl comes out of the cafe again behind him to serve the table next to me. Those are different people than who I saw come into the cafe earlier. Wait, she looks older too. She has longer and more pronounced features every-where. An doesn't seem to look much older. More of the same really. Still content as ever in this still weird and wild world we're still in.

"No, I'm okay. I've had enough."

Enough?

Why did I just say that?

Enough was the w– ... best word to add to your lexicon. It didn't mean the end was near. It meant... the beginning was near. It didn't mean you were finished. It meant YOU had... just started.

Enough? Ha! No. Yes. Enough... IS the answer. Enough is the only—

"Bao..." I call out.

Bao turned on his heel before walking away. "Yes, what is it, Tom?"

"What.. what day is it?"

"It's Monday, why?"

"Nothing." I smile, showing my teeth. Why am I smiling showing my teeth?

Bao nods and walks away and goes back into the cafe. He even moves like an older man.

For a second, I thought I just traveled through time as if I had been sitting in this chair for years, decades even. I go to grab my phone out of my pocket.

This isn't my phone. That's not the same background. Wait, that's me though? And that's Bao! And An!

I check the date on my phone. It HAD been years, nearly three years in fact, almost to the day that I arrived in Vietnam. I open up the front-facing camera on my phone. Holy shit, I have a beard! I look down at my waist, I've lost some weight. My hands feel more calloused and wrinkly than before, I must have been working.

An comes over to my table to refill my cup of iced tea. She smiles at me as she pours the tea gently and perfectly to the very top of the cup before it spills over.

"An, can I talk to you for a minute?"

"Yes, of course, Tom." She places the jug down and sits down next to me.

I'm trying to think of something to say where she would tell me what the hell I've been doing for the last 1,000 days in Vietnam without it seeming like I don't know what the hell I've been doing for the last 1,000 days in Vietnam.

"How is.... everything going?" I start talking without any plan for how to finish my sentence.

"I'm good. My back is a bit sore today. But, besides that, I'm good. And you?"

"Oh, yeah I'm fine." I'm not fine. I crumble.

"This is going to sound weird" I continue on, words spewing out rudderless, "but I feel like I've just come out of a daze. Like a coma. Like, you know, the Twilight Zone kind of thing." I'm trying to move with my hands conveying that my eyes have finally opened.

She smiles at me. It feels like I've seen that smile 10,000 times. Maybe I have? But nevertheless, it was like every time she smiled it was like the first time she ever used those muscles. It was a pure grin. One of true happiness. The grooves in her cheeks ran deep and a deep, endless current of joy coursed through her face.

"You know, when you first got here..." she took the bait, thank God, "you were a mess."

"A mess?" I say, a tad bit offended but quickly the tension in my shoulders released because I knew she was telling me the truth that I knew but didn't want to accept fully.

"Yes, a mess. Go here, do this. Let's go to the next place already. Why are we sitting around? Blah, blah, blah." She pours herself a glass of tea, again perfectly to the top and takes a sip. "Things were never enough for you. It seemed like you always wanted more."

My shoulders tense up again. More. Damn, I feel like I haven't thought about More in forever

I try to stoke the fire of conversation, "I know.. I know.. Do you think I've changed?"

"Oh, that's a tough question. Change? Do people really change? I feel like I haven't changed since I was a little kid. But you, yeah, I do. I do think you've changed Tom."

"How so?" I said recasting the line with more bait to keep the conversation going.

"It's difficult to say, but you seem much.... better now. I know before you had a big job that paid lots of money, but you hated it. Now, ever since you started working at the cafe with us, even if it's just sweeping the floor or cleaning the windows or even serving coffee sometimes, you seem... what's the word?" She takes another sip of tea. "Like you've out found how to enjoy having enough in life... Content. That's the word. You seem more content." She takes another sip of tea signalling that she's accomplished what she had to say.

Flashbacks begin raining down in my mind. So many days and nights at this cafe. So much conversation. So much laughing. So much sweeping and cleaning. So much time with Bao and An. So much coffee. But, I don't have any memories of speaking to the girl. It's been three years. Did I never talk to her once?

"And what about Chi?" I pause to search the rooms in my mind where I stored her name to see if there were any memories. "Chi" I repeat, "How's she?"

An laughs. "Oh Tom, you tell me. You're the one that's wanted to talk to her so much but never made a move. I saw her the other day while you were out. After the summer working with us, she returned for the new semester at school. She switched majors too, English to

Law. Thought she could make more money as a lawyer instead of being a teacher. She comes to the cafe to study sometimes but you're usually out running errands or sleeping or you're just..." She stopped.

"Just what?"

"I don't know. Scared?" She laughs again. "I know you like her, but to be honest, she's probably not your type."

"My type?" I laugh. "And what do you know about types?" I say trying to contain more laughter.

"I don't know." She returned the laughter. "I see on tv, everyone has a type. That's all."

Huh. This whole time I've been in Vietnam I've become a completely different person and didn't even realize it. And still, new or old, changed or not, I still haven't talked to Chi. Why? I ask myself but no answer comes to mind. I'll talk to her tomorrow and that's that.

"Oh, how many times have I heard that?" An laughs louder than before, finishes her tea and stands up to walk away. I did it again. Thinking out loud and talking to people.

"You'll see!" I say, laughing at myself knowing that it was probably true. I probably had said it every day for a 1,000 days without any attempts made at fulfilling my word. Traveling to a new country is easy when compared to starting a conversation with a girl.

I decided it was time to get some rest. An told me that my bed had been freshly cleaned and that if I wanted to lay down it was okay to go upstairs now. The hotel I thought I booked online must be a Bed and Breakfast above the cafe that Bao and An run. I walk up the stairs and open the door. The room was more empty than any other room

I ever had. It had a thin cot on the ground with one blanket and one pillow. A small stack of books — a Vietnamese language book, The Quiet American, Kitchen Confidential, The Old Man and the Sea, and a black notebook and a red pen. There are a few shirts hanging up inside a brown cabinet and one extra pair of pants on one side of the room. In the other corner, there was a door to the bathroom. There was a sink, a toilet, a towel rack, one of those water sprayers, and then a shower head in the corner.

It felt like home. It felt like more than enough for me.

I lay down on the cot, pull the blanket up to my chest, and scrunch the pillow under my neck. I can hear what sounds like karaoke in the distance. It was no matter. I was tired and I fell asleep instantly.

***

I wake up early in the morning and check my phone. 5:55. Some things never change. I get dressed and walk downstairs. Bao is wiping down the tables and An is sweeping the floors.

"Oh good, you're up," An says handing me the broom.

I take it and continue adding to the dust pile she had already started forming.

"Me and Bao need to go to the store. Do you need something?"

"I'm okay, thank you. I don't need anything," I say smiling.

Bao comes out from behind the cafe, "I did tables inside, do the outsides ones while we go to the store." I take the towel and throw it over my shoulder.

Before Bao and An leave, Bao turns around one last time, "Don't forget, Tom. The driver is out sick today. Has a fever and can't seem to smell anything either. So, he can't deliver the beans. Can you go to District 1 and pick them up?"

"Of course," I reply.

"Thank you, Tom," Bao said, handing me the keys.

I quickly swept up the rest of the cafe and wiped down the rest of the tables. It felt good to use my hands for something other than typing on a computer. I grab the key, put my shoes on, and walk out to the front of the cafe. Nobody had arrived at the cafe yet and there was only one bike there. This must be the bike. I start the bike and set off to pick up the coffee beans.

I tell myself, "I'll go get the beans and then when I come back, if Chi is there, I'm going to talk to her."

I peeled out of the cafe, took a right, and then another right, and then another right, and then realized I had no idea where I was going. I had no idea where District 1 was. I had no idea *what* District 1 was. Was it a store or street or place? For some reason, I felt like I was on the right road going the right way so I just kept driving. Despite how chaotic traffic is in Ho Chi Minh City, riding a motorbike is anything but. You're sitting still but still in motion. The tires are spinning but your head is not. Traffic somehow works even though one-way streets aren't and traffic lights are more like suggestions than rules. But oddly enough, everyone seems to be getting on just fine. I could feel my calloused hands on the exhaust. Gosh, it feels good to drive a motorbike. Beats having your hands around a steering wheel. What's that one book where he says,

"In a car you're always in a compartment, and because you're used to it you don't realize that through that car window everything you see is just more TV. You're a passive observer and it is all moving by you boringly in a frame. On a cycle the frame is gone. You're completely in contact with it all. You're in the scene, not just watching it anymore, and the sense of presence is overwhelming."

I remember the quote just not the book.... motorcycle something.

Whoa! Why is everyone slowing down? Break lights stretch across the road and begin to bottleneck with traffic veering left around something. What could it be?

I began driving slowly as I approach the crowd forming on the right side of the road. Holy shit. There's a body. Holy shit, there are three bodies. Holy shit, that's Bao and An!

I slam on the breaks and nearly crash myself. I kick the bike stand out and hop off my bike.

I start walking towards Bao first. He's staring right at me, right through me. Lifeless. He looked so much older than just yesterday. I wonder if on the last day on earth is the day you age the most? As if all the years that you were robbed of were sandwiched into one final spin of the Earth. I look over at An, her eyes closed. She looked as she always looked: content. She looked so much younger than just yesterday. Maybe I'm wrong. What if on the last day on Earth is the day that day you reverse aging to experience a taste of youth before you set off?

There I was again. Lost. Lost in a new layer of loneliness. Bao. An. My friends. No, my family. Gone. All gone.

I sat on the side of the road with Bao and An until the ambulance came and retrieved their bodies. The driver asked me for their identification and health insurance information. I told them I didn't know but I would go back to the cafe and look for it and bring it to the hospital. They agreed. So I got back on my bike and began retracing the streets back to the cafe.

I get to the cafe, park the bike, and see that there are a few people confused why nobody is in the cafe to serve them. I wave them off and go upstairs to find the right paperwork to help with Bao and An. In the room next to mine, the one I assumed was Bao and An's, I found a big box of paperwork. I still couldn't read Vietnamese so I just picked up the whole box and decided I'll take the whole thing with me and the people at the hospital can help me sort through the paperwork.

What the hell am I gonna do? Am I supposed to run this cafe now? I sweep the floors and clean the tables. I don't speak Vietnamese. What the hell am I gonna do? I couldn't stop repeating myself. The knot in my stomach kept twisting tighter and tighter. I walk downstairs with the box of papers, I look up, drop the box, and the papers spill out everywhere. It's Bill. Of all the people right now to see, it's fucking Bill.

"Tommy, buddy, what a treat seeing you here. How are you?" Bill said, plastering a smile on his face.

"Bill," I say, not knowing what else to say my best friend who had an affair with my wife and had nothing to do with me getting outed of my company that has my name on it. Well, my dad's name at least.

***

"You know there are a million coffee shops in this city, but for some reason, this one just screams Tom on it. I guess I got lucky finding you," Bill starts.

"What do you want, Bill?

"Look you have every right to be mad at me, all I want to do is talk for a minute. We've known each other for almost 20 years, give me five minutes."

"Look I don't have time for this right now, something happened....."

"Five minutes, Tommy. Please."

It was the first time in almost a decade of friendship that Bill ever said please to me. The last time was when his Dad died and he needed me to keep him company.

"Five minutes, then I really gotta go."

"Five minutes, that's it."

I quickly make him and me a cup of coffee. Why the hell am I making him coffee? The guy fucked my wife. Well, I don't really know why. Instincts, I guess. Maybe I have changed. Maybe in the midst of my daze, I moved on.

"Geez, they let anybody just walk behind the counter here to make their own coffee. What a country. You act like you own the place man," Bill said. He was trying extra hard to make an impression.

"I do own the place, Bill." That was a lie. But my instincts told me that I had to take responsibility for this place now.

"So it is true! You really did pack up everything, move to Vietnam, and open up your own coffee shop all because of watching a little Bourdain."

"I didn't open this shop. It was owned by...wait, what the hell do you know. Forget it. What do you want?

"Oh, relax. I'm here to see my best friend."

"Is that what we are.....best friends? Best friends don't ruin each other's lives," I said.

"Oh, that's water under the bridge by now isn't it Tommy, buddy? Besides look at yourself. You look way better than the last time I saw you. Have you quit drinking? You look leaner. Anyway,

I've come to make an offer. *An offer you can't refuse.*"

He was trying to impersonate The Godfather. Bill always did this when he was trying to take the air out of the room.

"Not interested."

"Oh come on, you haven't even heard the offer," he says. "Besides, Tommy you read Farewell to Arms. I know you did. Don't you remember? There is no escape."

"I know. I remember. And I'm not interested."

"Hear me out, Tommy, buddy. You can have your job back, VP corner office. Plus, a boost in salary once you talk it over with the board."

"The board," I scoff.

Bill continues on like he's some light at the end of the tunnel, some savior, like the second coming here to bail me out of my life. Bill isn't the light at the end of the tunnel, there is no light. If he's down there, it's just darkness.

"Corner office. Raise. A few new A shares, a few of mine to be exact. Oh, and we've expanded the business since you've been gone. We import coffee now. That's how I found you, more or less. We're hiring more staff too and opening up more offices," Bill's voice faded into the distance like a training passing by and through a tunnel in a mountain. He still seemed so far away.

It's the first time I heard that word in a long time. More.

Come to think of it, Bao never said it.

An never said it either.

I hadn't overheard it at the cafe this whole time.

If it was on any sign here in Vietnam, I didn't read it. I just realized I never even learned how to say it in Vietnamese. The word didn't exist in my world until now. Until it came out of Bill's mouth.

More.

The hairs on my neck begin to tango. Goosebumps race to fill my forearms. My eyes widen, and more light comes in. Smells, so many smells, have those smells always smelled like that on this street.

More. I haven't thought about the word in years. I felt like that girl getting stabbed by an adrenaline need in Pulp Fiction. I could feel the complexion in my face change, blood circulating through parts of my cheeks that haven't been touched in a while, like the grooves of an old river retaking shape after a drought. I realize that I've been staring at my reflection in the blackness of my coffee mug like the Greek God Narcissus. I look up at Bill.

"There he is," Bill said, with a genuine smile. One that says victory.

***

I chuckle, take a sip of my coffee, and lean back in my red stool, putting just enough pressure where I know the chair won't snap, "Tell me more."

Bill talked for more than five minutes but I didn't notice. A whole hour went by. I was intrigued. More trips around the world. More money. More opportunity. I was stuck in a daze, not in a sunken place but somewhere in the clouds.

"Oh shit," I stand up quickly. Things went a little fuzzy again. I'm dehydrated. Too much coffee, not enough water. I had completely forgotten about Bao and An. I tell Bill I'll think about it and race to the hospital. I go to the front desk to share their names. They point to the room they are in and....

It's too late. The doctor who speaks English told me that Bao and An were knocked into a coma for a little while and then passed away less than thirty minutes ago.

Where was I?

Talking to the guy that had ruined my life and had done it again.

I say my respects to Bao and An and then I'm ushered out of the building.

As I'm getting on my bike, Bill texts me to meet him at the airport. He had a flight booked for me to go back to the US.

I felt defeated. I felt like I failed.

I thought about what An had said earlier, "Do people change?"

I'm not sure I have.

Maybe on the surface, like my calloused hands from many mornings sweeping up the cafe, but deep down I was still a lot of the same. Maybe I was really just trying to sweep my old self under the rug so I could move on.

Maybe people don't change. I drove to the airport, parked the bike, and started walking toward the terminal.

People don't change, I told myself. Hell, I still walk around with my passport like before. You can't escape yourself. You are who you are. For better or worse. Wherever you go, there you are.

I got on my flight back to the US. Tan Son Nhat. Incheon. JFK. And away we go.... again.

When I stopped in Seoul for my layover, I had three hours to kill. I hadn't drunk a drop in almost three years but I broke that and guzzled three Jack n Coke's right there in the terminal, alone.

I fought back the tears that wanted to pour out of me.

"Travel around the world, you know, like Anthony Bourdain style or something like that. Check out Southeast Asia, that sort of thing."

I remember the words of the old man in the hotel with the cigarette-soaked walls. I wonder if he ever did go on that vacation. Maybe he died in that hotel room and the grim reaper bellhop served him his last meal. He was old after all. He didn't look like he had much left in the tank when I saw him that one time. How tragic that would be. To be old and not know when your last day is coming. If it's close or if you still have years to go and there are still things you always wanted to do but you never did.

We spend so much time tending to our daily checklist but tend very little to our life's bucket list.

And then one day, it's all gone.

I wonder what Bao and An still had left on their bucket list. I bet it was nothing. They learned early on the lesson of having enough.

Isn't it crazy that it takes your whole life of wanting and chasing more, only to learn that in the final analysis of it all, you had enough the whole time? That ever since the beginning, ever since you entered this world, you were enough. And that everything else was just extra, superfluous even.

I hiccup, and the Jack residue sends a cold shiver down my back, and goosebumps race from elbows down to my wrists. The PowerPoint. Bill's shiny forehead. The $3,000 suede ottoman. The dense air of my garage. Wiggles. The sunset. Sam. Syd. The old man. The red and white mint candies. Everything bubbled to the surface and flashed before my mind.

No.

I'm not going back.

Why?

Because I am enough.

I stand up, swallow my next hiccup, chug some water, go over to the airline desk and book a flight back to Ho Chi Minh City.

I'm taking over that cafe and I'm going to talk to Chi and that's that.

***

I step out of the airport and am once again greeted by a crop of waving arms asking me to take their taxi to wherever I wanted. I have done this before.

Good thing my bike was still there. I keep my head up and my hands loose as I sprint through the tunnel of people outside of Tan Son Nhat feeling the heat embrace me. I extend my arms in return. I had grown accustomed to the heat and it didn't slow me down. I got on my bike and started driving toward the cafe.

What the hell am I going to say to her? What if she doesn't speak English? What if she doesn't understand my embarrassing level of Viet-namese? What if she isn't Vietnamese and I just assumed she was this whole time? I don't know, but I just know I have to talk to her.

I get to the cafe, park my bike, run upstairs real fast to wash up and shake off the buzz from the Jack that was still lingering. I walk downstairs. Still no sight of her. I see some other locals so I serve them their coffee and grab a broom and start sweeping. If there's one thing I learned, it is that if I'm anxious don't just sit there and bounce your knee looking out the window. Put your hands to work. Make yourself useful. I swept the whole place and my mind was becoming clear. Then,

I grabbed a towel and began wiping down the empty tables. That's when I heard a bike pull up and park. It was her. She was here.

She looked even older than before and she didn't shuffle toward her seat. She walked confidently, gracefully, sure of herself. I saw she was holding a few textbooks. An wasn't lying. It seems she did really switch to wanting to be a lawyer and not wanting to be a teacher. She sat down at the table that I was at the other day. The same one I sat at when I first arrived in Ho Chi Minh City.

I wipe my hands off with the towel, toss it aside, grab the drinks menu, and make my way toward her table. She's already immersed in her book, highlighting passages, and folding the corner of pages. I place the menu on her table and she says,

"ya - mot cafe da khong duong."

Black coffee. No sugar. I say in my mind.

"Yeah – Mot cafe da khong duong," I repeat back, making my best attempt at the accent.

I don't know if my Vietnamese wasn't bad or was downright terrible, but I caught her attention. She laughed and looked up at me.

"Khong duong," she repeated. "No sugar," she added.

"No problem," I said back meekly. She smiles and returns to highlighting her book.

Nice, I thought. I can barely pronounce the words that are directly associated with running a coffee shop. Oh well, just make the damn coffee. And hey! She did smile. And she must know a little bit of English.

I go back to the cafe and pull out the glass bottle, unhook the top, and pour the black syrup-like concentration inside the glass over a bed of ice. I go to add sugar and stop. "Khong duong" I repeat to myself under my breath. I fill up a smaller glass with tea, place them on a silver tray and return to her seat.

She sees me coming over and closes her book as I place the tray on the table. As I'm placing the tea and coffee down, I notice the book says it's business law, more specifically international business.

"You're that guy that works for An and Bao?"

I was not expecting her to be the first to initiate a conversation.

"Uhh - yeah."

"The one that has wanted to talk to me, but never has."

"Uhh…" Thanks An.

"So, I'm here what would you like to say to me?"

I'm fumbling over my words. I never would have expected this directness. This level of confidence in a second language. She was primed to be a lawyer studying international business. She meant business.

"Umm, An told…tells me you're studying law," I didn't want to be the one to break the news.

"That's what you wanted to tell me? That An told you I'm studying law."

This is not going as expected.

I'm not sure what to say.

I just missed an international flight, on purpose, bought a new flight back to Vietnam, drove across the city tethered to unforgiving heat, and now this is how the conversation is going.

"Uhh....," still not sure what to say.

She lets a huge laugh. It startled me a bit. Her laugh, like her walk, was confident sounding. If that makes sense. Like I had followed her way exactly in the joke that she was pulling.

"I'm just kidding. I've wanted to talk to you, too."

"Really?"

"Yes, of course."

I sit down.

This is definitely not going how I expected.

"I have a question," she starts. She really does not wait for someone to initiate anything.

"You see that guy over there," she says looking past me to some other table.

My heart sinks a bit. First thing she points out is another guy in the room.

I turn around in my seat and notice another white guy sitting there. He looks like me. He looks like me when I traveled to all of those cities over the years. Drinking his coffee too fast. Flipping through the news-paper too fast. Declining calls. Answering texts. He looks uneasy. He looks unsatisfied. He looks like he's caught in the vortex of searching for More.

I know that guy. That guy is who I used to be and no longer am. Because now I am enough.

"Yeah, what about him?" I say, turning back to face Chi.

"What is your opinion of him?" she asks.

"He looks like he looking for More," I reply.

"What do you mean?"

"More. Doing more. Getting more money. Seeing more places. Being more."

"What's wrong with wanting more?" she asks puzzled. "Shouldn't a man strive for more in life?"

"Yes, but he doesn't know it yet but it will never be enough. If you're always chasing for more, that's all you'll ever do in life."

"And you - how about you? Are you not chasing for more in life? Isn't that what makes a 'true man'?" she asks again.

I laugh. I couldn't help it. I look at the coffee I just poured her, perfectly filled. I look at all the guests sitting in the cafe with its freshly swept floors and cleanly wiped tables. The bikes are whizzing by. The school kids are walking by. The heat is giving us a gentle hug. There's no more Jack on my breath. I feel the callouses on my hands. I had arrived.

"No. I have something he'll never have. Or at least he won't have until he goes his own way and learns it on his own."

"What's that?"

"I have enough."

"Enough?" she asks. Her confident tone was shattered. She was perplexed.

"I have enough already," I say with a big grin on my face. "I am enough."

"*Day du*," she says.

"What's that?"

"It means enough in Vietnamese"

"I like that," I reply. "*Day du*."

The End

Garrett MacLean

Garrett MacLean is the youngest in a big family from a small town in southern California called Fallbrook. He's lived, worked, studied, and traveled all over the world and has now lived in Ho Chi Minh City, Vietnam for nearly four years. He is a freelance writer, a podcast editor, an English teacher, an occasional poet, and is currently pursuing an online Master's degree in Journalism at New York University. This is his first complete short story.

The story is inspired by the parable "The Fisherman and the Business Man" written by the German writer Heinrich Theodor Böll. Yet, instead of being based off the coast of a small unnamed fisherman town in Europe, it revolves around a cafe in contemporary Saigon. The main character and first-person narrator, Tom, is defined by a simple idea: the pursuit of more. The story is of him discovering an even simpler idea: the thought of having enough.

CHAPTER 6

DE VECHTER

By

Thu Lan Anh Trang

Serik's hands were shaking when she picked up her cell phone from the table, blood from her nose dripped down on to the phone. Breathing was difficult as she searched for Tam's number on her contact list.

Serik was in a panic and anxious for Tam, her new Asian friend living in the same city with her, to answer the call.

Tam missed the call. Her family had arrived in Germany quite late so she was tired after the long drive. Tam was falling asleep while putting her daughter to sleep. Serik, crying hopelessly on the phone, left a voice message, "I need to talk to you now. Something bad happened. I need a friend to lean on." She stopped talking because she could not handle her emotions any longer.

...

Serik knew Tam from a welcome workshop organized by their city council for new immigrants. Serik was from Kyrgyzstan and could speak Russian, Chinese, English and Dutch. Both of them moved to the Netherlands at the same time. Their husbands were Dutch and they lived in a small city north of Rotterdam. They shared a lot with each other. For example, Serik did not have any children, but Tam had a two-year old daughter who she talked about a lot. Serik shared that she gave her husband a dog named Luke for his 40th birthday. They hung out often and talked almost every day.

Serik sent Tam a WhatsApp message, "Hey Tam, when are you back to the Netherlands? Can we see each other on Wednesday after you drop off your daughter at day care? I can come to your place."

Tam checked her phone, saw the message, and had a feeling that something had gone wrong. She replied quickly and tried to comfort Serik, "Hey dear, I'm worried about you. Yes. Let's catch up next Wednesday but please take care, ok? Let's me know what the bad thing was."

Serik did not respond immediately. After some hours, she wrote back, "I'll tell you more but, check out this photo."

Tam opened the WhatsApp file and saw the photo. Her face turned red. Tears fell on her chin with fear and her hands were shaking. She called Serik right away.

"Please tell me what happened? An accident? Or or...?"

Tam could not believe her eyes. The Serik in the photo had a bloody face. Her high-bridged nose was not straight anymore. Her left eye was purple and it looked like she could not open it. The eyelid was so swollen. There were some marks on Serik's face and neck. Tam tried not to think of domestic violence while Serik sobbed on the phone.

"Yes, he. It was him. He did that to me."

"No, no way. How could he do that? What actually happened? Tell me?"

"That bastard hit me this morning. I hate him. I hate him," Serik yelled on the phone. "He should go to the hell. I can't forgive him."

Tam could not say a word. She sat quietly and slowly on the leather couch in the living room of her uncle's old house. She did not feel that the couch was comfortable anymore and she was frightened.

"Serik, calm down. Breath in, breath out. I'm with you."

"Please. Let's catch up next week when you're back. I need you."

Serik stopped talking, sighed, and then she hung up the phone. She left a text message for Tam, "I'm going to try to sleep now. I'll tell you in detail next week. Just enjoy the time with your family. I'll get better soon."

After a few minutes of thinking of what to write, Tam wrote an encouraging message in Dutch.

"Serik, luister, je bent een vechter." (Translation: Serik, listen, you are a fighter)

...

The time of Covid was not easy for anyone. Since the pandemic started in early 2020, everything changed in the Netherlands. Life seemed to be harder with lockdowns, curfews, and the fear of being infected. Office workers like Serik and her husband Noah were asked to work from home. Restaurants, bars, cafes, fitness centers, and stores were forced to close. People's lives were kept at home, within their own walls. People who lived in a house might have more space with a garden or a backyard even if it was small. For those who lived in small apartments like Serik and Noah, it was more difficult because they were stuck with just four walls and they had to see their partners 24 hours a day.

Before the pandemic hit the country, their married life was full of happiness and laughter. Even though Serik was vegetarian, she still cooked good food with meat or seafood for her husband after she returned home from work. Noah helped her with the housework and took care of their dog Luke. Serik viewed her marriage through rose-colored glasses. Noah was the best husband and choice for her. She thought that marrying him was the best decision that she had ever made.

They wanted to enjoy their life so they decided not to have children before they turned 40 years old. Both of them tried hard to build up their careers. Noah worked for a technology company while Serik was a writer at a media company. Over dinner, they always shared with each other about their work. They talked about everything that was happening during the day. It seemed that there were no secrets between them.

However, their conversations became less and less during the months when the Netherlands was in Covid lockdown and they had to work from home. They had arguments over things not even remotely related to them such as something from the news. They looked seriously at the weaknesses of the other. Serik could easily complain to Noah when she found dirty cups and plates in the sink. Noah was mad when he found out that Serik did not place the vacuum cleaner in the same the position where he usually put it. Their life got more difficult as the lockdowns increased and they could not go out or give themselves any private space or time.

Noah did not like sports so he could not entertain himself with any activity during Covid except to play video games. He did not have many friends due to his introverted personality. He could not see the close friends that he had or his family as often as before. He established a barrier around him that no one could break through. He refused to contact his friends either via social media or over the phone. He only talked to his parents when they called him. His life was only with Serik, Luke, the television, his laptop, and video games, any kind of video games.

Serik chose to avoid unnecessary conversations that would lead to arguments. Instead, she pursued outdoor sports such as running during the lockdown when all the sports centers were closed. When there were no strict restrictions, she went back to golf and tennis. She tried to connect to her community again and socialize as much as she could. She did not want to stay at home all the time, but they were still encouraged to work from home.

...

One day, Serik came home from the golf course, dragging her golf bag, and left it in front of the storage closet. She sat down tiredly on the couch, closed her big eyes, and tried to nap. She thought of the argument that she had with her husband that morning. When Noah was mad and told her that she was useless, Serik froze. She did not believe his behavior recently. She opened her big brown eyes and looked at him with tears. This was not the first time they had an argument since working from home due to the pandemic.

Her long dark hair was a mess after a long day at the golf course and it covered her beautiful face. She had a typical beauty of a Central Asian woman in her mid-30s. That was why Noah fell in love with her at first sight when they met at the University of New South Wales a few years ago. Serik was not only beautiful, but also smart and talented. Noah could not take his eyes off of her. He was impressed with Serik's language ability. He had never met any women who could speak more than three languages before but Serik did really well with English, Russian and Chinese.

However, everything changed because of Covid.

Serik spent more and more time with sports and her lifestyle activities in order to avoid seeing her husband 24 hours a day. When the lockdown finished and sport centers were allowed to open again, she immediately registered for golf, tennis, and the gym. Noah did not like sports at all. He just wanted to play video games instead of going out. Serik therefore chose to go out. During the lockdown when everything was closed, Serik went jogging every morning for at least one hour before starting work.

Noah opened the door, took his shoes off, and rolled his blue eyes when seeing Serik's golf clubs blocking his way. He wanted to swear but Luke came running to him which made him relax and smile happily. "Hello, Luke. Did you miss me?" Serik saw him going into the kitchen with Luke then she left for the bathroom.

Noah gave Luke some food and then he came back to Serik's golf clubs. Noah opened the door of the storage closet and loudly threw the golf clubs into it. He was quite big for the small storage space so he did not want to go inside. Serik heard the sound and she was scared. She knew he might start a fight if she was out there. Noah talked in Dutch with a hard voice, "If you leave your stuff out like this, I'll throw them out to the street." Serik sobbed under the shower. She did not know why she was so sensitive. Noah was not this kind of person two years ago or this might be his true personality but she did not know it. She knew what she would submit to her boss for publishing next week: How people had changed during Covid. She turned off the water, dried herself, and went out of the bathroom. She would write this column before she forgot.

Noah sat on the couch, watching TV, while the food he bought from the supermarket was in the oven. He did not want to have dinner with Serik tonight so he made some meat for himself. Serik also tried to avoid seeing him with the excuse of working. It was a good excuse for both of them so they wouldn't be at the same dining table.

However, Noah could not control his temper when Serik walked into the study room and ignored him. He approached her while she was closing the door.

"I need to talk," Noah yelled at Serik.

"I must work now. Can we talk later when I finish this column? I have to submit it by tomorrow morning."

"No. I need to talk," Noah repeated. His face turned red and he looked like he could break the door down if Serik did not allow him in.

"Okay! What do you want to say?"

"You must sit at the table to have dinner with me. I bought some vegetarian food from the supermarket for you."

"I don't like ready-to-eat food from the supermarket. You know that, don't you?"

"I said: Have dinner now. Don't make me repeat it. Now!"

"I said no," Serik replied to him firmly.

Noah took some deep breaths and he quickly came closer to Serik. He held her left hand and pulled her towards the living room.

Serik screamed, "Stop! You're hurting me. Let go of me."

Noah could not stand it anymore. He was exploding inside. He pushed Serik to the wall, held her hand hard, and squeaked, "You're my wife. You must listen to me."

"I'm your wife, not your slave. Let go of me."

Noah did not listen to Serik. He could not control himself. He slapped her face and then punched her right eye. Serik screamed out loud, "Bastard. Stay away from me. I hate you."

She tried to run away from him but he was too strong for her to escape. He held her wrist so hard that it turned red. He pulled her hair and dragged her back when she tried to move to the front door. She wanted to go out and call for help. He pushed her back to the wall. He punched her one more time on the nose causing blood to spurt out.

Serik was in severe pain. She cried out, "Help me, help me" but she was in too much pain to make it loud. Her voice was soft and weak.

Noah saw that Serik's face was full of blood and he was scared. He spoke in a low voice, "I'll take you to the hospital. Come on!"

He put on his jacket and then took Serik's jacket and put it on her. Serik could not move due to the pain. She covered her face with both hands and cried. Noah helped her stand up and they left the apartment. Luke hid himself somewhere in the living room. He had witnessed everything. It was in the middle of autumn but Serik felt like it was winter already. She leaned on the wall of the building while waiting for Noah to hail a car. She felt cold with just an autumn jacket. She thought she needed a thicker coat. Her nose did not stop bleeding.

It was only a 10-minute drive to the hospital yet it felt like hours. No one said a word. They maintained their silence and panic. Serik went straight to the emergency room. With their experience, the doctor and nurses suspected something bad had happened to this woman. After giving Serik first aid, the doctor asked, "How do you feel now? Your nose will get better after a few hours so no need to worry too much. The purple circle on your eye may be there for a few days or a week. Are you a victim of domestic violence?"

Serik did not know what to say. If she admitted it, they would call the police and Noah would be in trouble. If she kept silent, she might suffer more from Noah's violence. This seemed to be the beginning of his terrible behavior. She remembered what she learned from the workshop organized by the city council, "If you don't speak up, you will continue to be the victim and the cruel action won't stop." She knew she would be protected, and she would have to be brave to raise this issue.

"Yes. My husband beat me. He hit me on the face, not only once."

"We'll call the police. Are you okay to report this to them when they're here?"

"Yes. I will."

...

When Serik felt better, she called a taxi to go home. Noah was still at the police station. After the police recorded the case from Serik, they took Noah with them for more investigation. Serik knew, of course, that they would add this to Noah's criminal file. At that point in time, she wished he would be kept in jail so that he would pay for what he did.

The apartment was empty. Luke was still hiding behind the plant in the living room. Serik felt so cold and she did not want to stay any longer in the living room. She was exhausted and in pain. She got changed and stayed in the bedroom with the door closed and the lights out. She sat on the edge of the bed and tried to empty her mind but could not.

When Serik was a little girl living in Kyrgyzstan, she saw the gender inequalities there and she thought her life in Europe would not be like the women in her country. She studied abroad and experienced what people call freedom in Australia. She knew that her life had changed. She fell in love with her husband, a gentle Dutch man, an exchange student, had a beautiful wedding, and then moved to the Netherlands, a country that values freedom and equality. Her friends back home were jealous. Serik seemed to have everything that she desired when she was young: a good husband, a nice life in a beautiful country, and a dream job.

However, everything turned into a disaster after just two years. Well, it is more accurate to say that Covid had changed everything. She was stuck at home, had no communication, and suffered violence from Noah. Serik could not hold back her tears. It was painful for her to cry even though her nose had stopped bleeding after the doctor stitched up the wound. She sat quietly and miserably on the bed, holding her knees, thinking about all the things she expected, and all the things that had happened.

She was still frightened when Noah knocked on the door and asked softly, "Babe, are you all right? Can I cook something for you or do you want some take away seafood?"

Serik was in a panic. Her heart beat so fast. She was afraid that Noah would enter the room without her permission and hit her again. She did not know how to respond. She pulled the blanket over herself and pretended that she was asleep already. Noah came closer to her, sat on the edge of the bed, and sighed slightly, "It is cold inside. You may not sleep well with this temperature. I'll turn on the heater for you. Let's have a nap. I'll order some food."

Serik replied softly and interruptedly, "I'm so tired and in pain. I cannot breathe normally now. I just want to sleep."

Noah left the room quietly. Serik felt empty. Since he came home from the police station, he did not apologize to her for anything. He acted like he did not hurt her. Serik was anxiety-ridden and questioned herself, "How could he behave like this? I did not want this kind of life." She cried again, painfully.

In her country, there might be inequality and women did not have as much power as men, but her father never hurt her mother. Her brother-in-law never used violence or even slapped her sister. Her father always educated her younger brother to be a gentle man. She could not imagine that she suffered from domestic violence in an equal country where women had a lot of power and protection. What made her even more scared was Noah's attitude and manner. He did not regret what he did to her.

Serik felt the dryness in her throat. She walked stealthily to the door and half-opened it to check out Noah first before going out to grab a bottle of water in the kitchen. She saw Noah sitting on the couch, relaxing, and playing happily with Luke. Serik felt like someone had crushed her heart. Noah stroked Luke and said sweetly to him, "Do you feel better now? Sorry that we scared you today. Don't be afraid. I'll protect you, my baby."

His action and words broke her heart. Maybe he loved the dog more than his wife. He felt sorry about scaring his dog, but it was okay to hit his wife.

...

Serik met Tam on the following Wednesday when Tam came back from Germany. They sat in a quiet café on a busy street of Rotterdam. Everyone was still afraid of Covid-19 as infections rose significantly every day and a new variant had appeared. The sky was grey and it looked like heavy rain was coming. They were by the window where they could see the seasons change. This was the color of autumn and most of the red leaves would be gone by the end of this month. Winter would come with the bad weather, the darkness, and the sadness.

"Autumn is sad enough, isn't it? We don't have to wait until winter to feel it," Serik said breaking the ice to start a conversation.

Neither Serik or Tam wore makeup since they had to wear masks all the time. There was no point except for the eyes. Serik's eyes were beautiful. She put the make-up on to cover the purple circle from Noah's punch even though it was less visible now.

"Would you mind if I take off my mask?" Tam asked.

"Oh, no problem."

Both of them took their masks off and Tam was shocked when seeing Serik's nose. There was still a mark on her nose and it was easy to see that someone had beaten her up.

"Serik, your nose? Oh my God! Was it an accident?"

"No. It wasn't. He, ah... Noah did this to me. He did it on the day I called you."

At that moment, Tam just wanted to give Serik a hug. She thought she could understand how much Serik hurt. She did not know how to respond. She held Serik's hands and said, "It's over. I'm back. You have me by your side."

Tam dragged the chair next to Serik and put her hands on Serik's shoulders. Serik felt more comfortable and started telling Tam about the incident. Her voice was weak but she had no fear anymore.

Tam could not say a word after the story. Now it was her turn to be frightened. She could not imagine that her friend had suffered from these terrible things. It was even worse than what she thought when reading Serik's message. Serik felt better now that she could open the wound to share with others. She felt that the rock on her chest had been lifted and so she could breathe again.

"Why don't you move to a safe house to stay away from him?" Tam asked

"I will leave the country next week for a few months to visit my family in Kyrgyzstan. Maybe I can get over it completely. He has not harmed me now. He acts like nothing happened, but I can't," Serik dragged a half-smile out of her lips. "Ridiculous, right? I'm living with the one who used violence on me. Sometimes I don't understand myself very well. Yesterday, he was so sweet to me. At that moment, I thought we can start over and pretend nothing bad was there. I'm such a loser. I'm still in love with him."

"Well, don't blame yourself for being that weak. Emotion isn't easy to clear. But I think you should move out. You never know."

"I'm sure I will move out and look for somewhere to stay after coming back. At least it's not too difficult for me to return to Kyrgyzstan during this time. Self-quarantine is fine for me. I just wanna spend time with my family because I haven't seen them for two years. Working from home isn't that bad aye?"

"When you're away, I'll look around to see if there are any vacant apartments for rent and let you know."

"Thanks so much," Serik looked into Tam's eyes with gratitude. She did not tell her colleagues or other friends about this. Tam was the only one whom she shared and looked for support.

They let the silence lead the conversation as no word would be as powerful as sitting side by side to feel the sympathy. The coffee in their cups turned cold. They looked through the window of the café to watch people walking by and rushing to stay dry from the coming rain. The wind blew dry leaves on the ground and up into the air. The rain started falling.

...

The following week, Serik entered the business lounge at the airport. It was the first time for her to be there. She indulged herself with a fancy trip back home. Serik found an empty table next to the food station and sat down. She was a bit tired. She had to take the metro and then a train to the airport. Noah refused to drive her. Serik looked around to feel the ambience and said to herself, "Damned Noah! It's worth a long trip to be here. Hmm why do I have to be a cheap ass to myself?" She could not find any reason for her to save money now so she spent quite a lot for the business class ticket to Kyrgyzstan. It was pretty busy in the lounge and not easy to find a table. She was so happy to have somewhere to sit and start working while waiting for the flight.

Serik went to the food and drink station to grab some snacks, fruit, and a glass of wine. When she came back to her table, she saw a man standing by her table with a clumsy and awkward manner.

"Oops, sorry. I didn't know this is your table," he said.

"Well, I can't sit on all three chairs so you can sit here if you want."

"Thanks so much. If you don't mind, may I sit here?"

Serik nodded her head and invited him to share the table. The man put his laptop on the table and introduced himself, "My name is Henk van Den Berg. I'm from Utrecht. Excuse my mask and inability to shake your hand."

Serik laughed but she did not know if Henk noticed that because her face was hidden under the mask too.

"I'm Serik Smit from Rotterdam. Well, I'm originally from Kyrgyzstan and I changed to my husband's surname but just call me Serik," she said.

Even though Serik could not see Henk's face, she could guess that he was around 50 due to his eyes and grey hair. He had the typical height of a Dutch man. She thought he would be taller than 1.90m. Henk also noticed this woman with some mysterious attraction even with her mask on. He could only see her eyes and her sexy body under the tight sweater and skinny jeans. It was casual but appealed to him and he could not keep his eyes off of her.

Both of them sat opposite to each other for 30 minutes, focusing on their work laptop, and did not communicate much except greetings. Serik closed her laptop, looked at her watch, packed everything into her bag, and then stood up. She smiled at the stranger who was her companion for 30 minutes.

"Hey, I gotta go. My flight will be boarding soon. I must get to the gate. Nice to meet you, Henk"

"Err, ah, nice to meet you, too," Henk said, a little bit surprised that he had no idea how to respond.

Serik waved at him, took her travel bag, and left. Henk was kind of awakening now. He ran after her with his name card and cell phone, "Serik, um, Mrs. Smit, this is my name card. Drop me a line on any type of means from WhatsApp to imessage."

"Thanks, but I don't have my name card. Sorry!" Serik opened her bag and realized she did not bring any name cards.

"Ah you can ring to my phone so that I can save your number, if you don't mind," Henk looked down at his shoes. He had no idea why he had no confidence in front of this woman.

"Sure thing," Serik replied eagerly.

Then Serik skimmed through his name card to seek the number and called him. She also found out that Henk was a businessman and she thought, "Hmm, that's quite interesting!"

"Aha, you got my number, right? Be in touch and have a safe flight!" said Serik and then she turned her back to walk out of the door with her carry-on. Henk still stood there and looked at her as Serik was walking straight to her gate without turning back to check him out. Henk thought, "This woman is really sexy and interesting." Henk could not see Serik's face but her attitude and confidence drew his attention. Women were usually attracted to him before he to them. Serik was different.

...

Quality time with family was always wonderful. Despite the pandemic, Serik still enjoyed being with her parents, brothers, and sisters at home. She could not see many friends due to the restrictions and people were scared of Covid but she was happy to sleep in her own bed and talk on the phone with friends and relatives any time she wanted to without worrying about the time difference.

One morning as Serik sat in the garden, she got a WhatsApp message from Henk. He was on a business trip to the U.S for a week to buy a winery. He told Serik how warm California was compared to his home country. Serik laughed joyfully when hearing his stories. She wished she could travel to the U.S to see the vineyard and taste the wine. She told him about Hunter Valley in New South Wales, Australia which was her favorite place to visit wineries.

It made Serik wonder why she did not meet Henk before and dated him instead of Noah. Perhaps Noah was only a university sweetheart. He had nothing before they got married. He had a normal and boring job. They rented an old apartment and she had to pay half the cost of a car which she never used because she had no driver's license. They split their bills for everything even their holidays. She had to admit that love was blind and now she seemed to regret it.

Serik stayed with her parents for almost three months. They wanted her to stay longer, but she decided to go back to the Netherlands. She did not intend to tell her family what happened, but her parents sensed something was wrong.

"Serik, please tell us. What happened?" her father said.

"Nothing," Serik replied.

"We saw you crying when you were talking with your aunt about equality and freedom in Holland. There must be something wrong for you to have that kind of emotion."

"Well, I intended to hide this from you but...hmm, Noah hit me. He hit me hard enough to be in the hospital."

"No way! How dare him? I will kill him," shouted Serik's father.

Serik's mother held her face with both hands and cried, "My little girl! No, no, I can't imagine. You're our treasure and we always gave you the best. Why? How come that guy beat my little girl? Unbelievable! It happened in that country where they praise gender equality. In our family, nothing like that happened. Never! None of women in this family were mis-treated."

As Serik told her secret, they told her about their time staying with Noah and her when they visited the Netherlands.

Prior to the pandemic, they already had a feeling that something was not right. Serik was still in the throes of love. They told her that Noah did not show proper behavior to them back then. Serik could not believe what she heard. He told her parents to get out of his apartment and even threw their stuff out the door. They did not tell Serik because they thought it would affect her relationship.

"Sorry mom and dad," said Serik. "You had to suffer because of me. Everything will change. I promise. I'll be stronger and when I visit you next time, it will be a different me. I must go back there because I need the Dutch passport. I'm almost there. I only have a few months left."

···

Serik returned to the Netherlands after the New Year celebrations with her family. Noah did not pick her up from the airport even though she called him with her arrival dates. Serik dragged her luggage to the arrival hall mindlessly wondering how she could get home with all the bags. Suddenly, she bumped into someone. She looked up and saw it was Henk.

"What are you doing here?" she said with surprise.

"What a coincidence that I arrived at the same time as you," said Henk. "I've just come back from Spain, well, my vacation." Henk smiled warmly to her. "May I give you a lift? I parked my car at the airport car park. It's not too far a walk."

"Oh, really? Is it possible? Thanks so much," Serik said as he took care of her heavy suitcases.

···

Noah looked up the clock on the wall and guessed that Serik had arrived but he had no intention of picking her up from the airport. He did not want to go out in the cold and wet weather. He initially thought he might surprise her at the airport, but then he changed his mind. As a man who had been away from his wife for a few months, he definitely wanted her though and would push her into bed. This thought motivated him to text her that he would pick her up from the train station.

While he checked the weather again, he saw a fancy Tesla stopping at the entrance of their building. A tall man stepped out and opened the car door and his wife stepped out. He could not believe his eyes. He just wanted to go downstairs and put some marks on that guy's face with his fist. He did not know what to do so he picked up Luke to help him calm down.

Serik opened the door and found Noah sitting on the couch, holding Luke, and watching Formula One. She tried to say something to break the ice, but Noah did not care. Serik brought her suitcases to the living room and then went to the bathroom. She had gotten wet from the rain. Noah stared at her and realized that she was really sexy with wet hair. His male instincts asked him to do something because this was his wife and, to him, she was his asset. He could do whatever he wanted to her and she must please him.

Noah approached Serik from behind and put his arms around her belly and then moved his hands higher. Serik was quite shocked and frightened. She tried to say something but he was so quick to push her against the wall. Serik had no power at all. She did not react, but her tears came out. It was not pleasure but pain. Serik now understood the feeling of the women whom she had interviewed for her column describing forced sex.

After that incident, Serik called Tam and told her what happened. Tam advised her to report it to the police, but Serik rejected that. For her, Noah was still her husband so she did not think she should do that.

"Maybe you still love him," asked Tam.

Serik replied with a half smile, "Or maybe not. I am thinking more about my citizenship."

Tam knew what she meant as she was also in the process of applying for a Dutch passport. If Serik divorced now, she might lose everything and have no chance to stay.

...

After Serik came back to the Netherlands, she and Noah fought almost every day. Noah easily lost his temper for the simplest of reasons. One day, he asked Serik to let Luke sleep on their bed but Serik refused. She loved the dog and treated him like their kid, but she could not imagine that she would sleep next to Luke in bed. Noah exploded in anger, stepped closer to Serik, and tried to slap her. Fortunately, she could avoid his hand.

"Stop using violence against me. You must end this. Otherwise, I'll call the police," Serik shouted.

"DON'T...ever...challenge me," Noah said.

"I don't threaten you. I'll do it, if you dare me," Serik could not stand it anymore. She was like a balloon that was about to explode.

Noah stopped and punched his fist against the wall. He leaned his forehead on the wall and exhaled. Serik's body was shaking and she was trying to keep her eyes closed when her phone rang. It was her boss. He called to remind her to show up on time for an interview with a politician from the Liberal party of Rotterdam. She was supposed to write a story about this new young and talented leader. Without saying anything, Serik grabbed her bag, checked her make-up, put on a coat and her boots, and then left Noah who was standing still in the apartment.

After she was gone, Noah grabbed a bottle of beer from the fridge, sat down on the couch, and drank it all in one big gulp. His eyes were still red with the anger. He needed to release it in some way. He held up the empty bottle for a couple of minutes and then threw it at Serik's favorite Delft blue vase. It broke into pieces. Noah held his head with both hands and exhaled. Luke ran away quickly to the study room and stayed there for the rest of the afternoon.

...

Serik met Max Wilde for the first time at his office in Rotterdam and he made a good first impression. He was considered as a potential candidate for the leadership position in his party. He was in his mid-40s, successful in politics, and had received a lot of attention from the media. It took a while for Serik's company to arrange this interview, especially conducting it in English. If she did not know his name, she would have thought he had been born in an English speaking country. Serik had to admit to herself that she was attracted by his charm, gentlemanly manner, and intelligence.

"Thank you, Mr. Wilde for the interview. I'm sure that a good story about you will be released soon and before the election," Serik said in Dutch.

"Oh, that would be great! I'm quite impressed with your Dutch. How long have you been here, Mrs. Smit?" Max said with a bright smile.

"Almost three years and I've been with my company for almost two years," Serik answered clumsily though she had no idea why she said that. She said to herself, "Shit! What's wrong with you, Serik? Why didn't you say something smarter than that?"

"Interesting! Anyway, thanks for coming to my office and watch out for the weather. I bet rain is coming," said Max showing his diplomatic manner while looking outside at the grey sky.

"Oh no! I forgot my umbrella," Serik bit her lips as she looked out the window. She was not aware that Max was watching her. He reckoned that this Central Asian woman was not only smart but also attractive. She appealed to him in a strange way that he had never experienced before even though he met many people from Central Asia due to his work.

"Ah, take this umbrella with you and make sure you don't get wet," Max handed his umbrella to Serik with a cheeky smile. She looked at him with a gratitude.

"Thank you! I'll return it to you next time," Serik said. They shook hands and she left the office. On the way out of the building, Serik could not get his image out of her mind, especially his cheeky smile.

On the metro back home, she kept thinking of what would happen if she tried to seduce Max, a never-married man with high social status and education. Is it unprofessional or acceptable? She considered some scenarios and turned the umbrella around and said, "You'll be the reason for a second appointment."

...

When Serik arrived at her home station, the rain started pouring down. While under her umbrella and walking home, she suddenly stopped and checked her bag for the house key and realized she had left her keys inside the apartment. She had no choice but to call Noah and ask him if he could pick her up at the station. Noah hung up the phone on her. It was almost 6.30pm and she was caught in the heavy rain. The umbrella did not help that much. She knew that Noah would not let her in the apartment until his anger was gone. She had to find somewhere to stay until Noah received her call and agreed to open the door for her. She remembered that Tam's house was nearby.

Tam opened the door and saw that Serik was soaking wet.

"Oh dear! What's wrong? Come on in. It's cold outside. Quick!" she said.

Tam asked her husband to bring a towel for Serik and offered her a cup of tea. Serik noticed that they were having some guests sitting around the dining table. She stepped back to the entrance hall and told Tam that she should leave. She did not know that Tam had guests.

"No worries! Let's go upstairs first to dry yourself off and get changed," Tam took Serik upstairs to change and asked her what happened. Serik could not hold back her tears. She sobbed and told Tam everything about Noah and all the fights they had.

"Ah! What a coincidence that you're here!" replied Tam. "Come on. Let's go downstairs. I'll introduce you to someone who might be interesting for you. I have an idea."

Serik did not know who Tam wanted to introduce but she could see the excitement in Tam's eyes. Serik dried her hair, tidied it up a bit, checked her face, removed some mascara around the eyes, put on her lipstick, and then followed Tam downstairs. She looked stunning in Tam's dress. Luckily, they wore the same size clothes.

"Hey, An, this is Serik Smit. She is living in this city but she's working for a media company in Rotterdam. Serik is as new to the country as me," Tam laughed. "Serik, this is An Janssen Le, my Vietnamese friend living in Amsterdam. An is a feminist, living here for 20 years or so. This is her husband, Floris Janssen, a lawyer. Well, it's a silly introduction aye?" Tam laughed and continued. "I think that you guys might do something together. Ah, I forgot the most important man, my husband, Albert."

The introduction broke the ice and everyone laughed. They sat down around the dining table and continued their dinner. Tam told An about Serik's story and then shared with Serik An's idea of establishing an open house for foreign women who were the victims of domestic violence. They could stay in the house temporarily if they were unable to find somewhere to move out to. That house would also be the place to host some skills training and language teaching for any foreign women who recently migrated to the Netherlands and were looking for a community like that.

Serik really loved the idea and immediately linked it to some contacts that might help them with setting it all up. The biggest issue was how to find a house during this difficult time with Covid. Serik immediately thought of Henk. Perhaps he could help.

...

Serik, Tam, and An decided to set up an NGO, a non-governmental organization, to help victims of domestic violence. They came up with a detailed plan and a proposal to pitch to Henk van Den Berg for a location. Serik invited Henk out for lunch at an Italian restaurant for the pitch. Of course, Henk accepted the invitation without a second thought.

Henk looked at the woman sitting in front of him with admiration. She was not only beautiful, but also smart and ambitious. He did not believe that she and her partners could come up with this kind of proposal. It was beyond his expectations, especially for newcomers like them. He was impressed with the way she presented the plan and with their passion and seriousness. When she finished her presentation, Henk nodded his head with a mysterious smile.

"Hey, has anyone told you that you look amazing when you're serious?" Henk said cheekily.

"Has anyone told you that you look charming when you say yes to my proposal?" Serik replied in a funny way but she, too, looked straight into his eyes.

"Well, I have to admit that I can't say no to an attractive woman with a wonderful plan for the community. Come to my office tomorrow. My assistant will arrange an appointment for you to take a look at some of my properties across the country. I suggest a house in a rural area with a farm so that you can have a big place with something to do with it. What do you reckon?"

"Absolutely perfect! I don't know what I should say. Thanks so much for your generosity!" Serik's eyes were bright with hope and happiness.

"Just to let you know that I offer this because of you, gorgeous!" Henk always called Serik like this in messages or over the phone. Serik sometimes felt a bit embarrassed but she also liked it. Henk was the kind of man that every woman would desire to have in their lives.

Going home after the meeting with Henk, Serik could not hide her excitement and happiness. She started comparing Henk and Max without any intention. Noah had no position in that comparison. Max drew her attention from the first time they met and she could not stop thinking about him, but the more she interacted with Henk in person, the more she was impressed, a successful businessman with a kind heart for society.

...

Tam helped Serik find a small studio so she could move out. She could not stand being around Noah's unstable manner anymore. They did not talk to each other and he only showed his long face and hot temper. They easily started fighting about the smallest of things. Serik wanted to stay away from that. If she stayed with Noah any longer, depression would set in. She did not want to suffer from physical and mental abuse anymore. This was the time for her to stay strong and positive, otherwise she could not help anyone else. When she told Noah that she would move out, he did not say anything. He just asked her if she wanted a divorce. Serik did not think about the divorce yet since she still wanted Dutch citizenship. She avoided giving him an answer and that made him crazy. He yelled at her, threw her stuff out of their apartment, and pushed her out.

...

Serik knew it was not professional to ask Max out for dinner but she wanted to see him again and introduce her new project. He could be really helpful with promoting her organization. It was called VRIENDINEN which translates to 'Girlfriends' in English. They named the organization like this to remind women that they always had some girlfriends who were willing to help them like sisters. At this stage of the NGO, she needed lots of support from any source she could find.

Max did not expect Serik to call him and invite him out with the reason of returning his umbrella. But whatever it was, he wanted to see this woman again. The more he knew about this woman, the more he was attracted to her. With his experience, he knew that she was interested in him too but she definitely tried to keep a distance in order to be professional. Additionally, her project sounded potentially interesting for him and he could draw more attention from this kind of group when it came to the election. Also, Max and Serik would have more time working together, but neither of them mentioned this though they each thought about it.

Quite quickly, VRIENDINEN became well-known in the community. They gave shelter to immigrant women who were victims of domestic violence, helped them with their legal documents, skills and language training, and provided job assistance. The organization grew fast and more opportunities arose for them. Serik was the key person for VRIENDINEN due to her passion and ambition. Over the weekends, they hosted classes for other foreign women who wanted to learn Dutch or cooking, baking, and some other skills. They had more volunteers to help and the house turned out to be a nice place for women in the community no matter whether they were foreign or Dutch. They built a garden together, enjoyed tea time or lunch, and studied about other cultures. The network expanded quickly.

Serik and Noah separated, but Noah knew Serik's weak link, Dutch citizenship. It was almost time for Serik to obtain a Dutch passport but what if she was divorced? Noah called Serik one day to ask her to come back to the apartment to collect her stuff. Her project was growing and Serik knew it would be a pity if she had to leave, but she did not want to be abused anymore. She found her self-confidence again and she made a plan that if she had to leave the Netherlands, she would still roll out her NGO model in other countries or even back home. Serik was not afraid of Noah anymore and it was time to face him. Divorcing him was the way to release herself from that horrible marriage and she might even start her life over with either Henk or Max.

Serik sat quietly on the couch as Noah put a paper on the table and told Serik that if she wanted to divorce she should just sign it, but that she might lose everything.

"Take it or leave it! Your choice. If you sign the paper, your life in the Netherlands is over. You must get out of this country. If you apologize to me, you can come back to this place," he said.

"You think I have everything with you, don't you? Never over-estimate yourself. I'm fed up," Serik said with a half-smile.

"How dare you," said Noah as he came closer to Serik. "DON'T ever look down on me! IF you want to stay in Holland, come back and please me. Be a good wife. Close your f*king NGO. That really irritates me."

"Stop it! I'll scream and the neighbors will call the police. Stay away from me," Serik shouted.

Noah did not listen. He grabbed her wrist and dragged her to the couch. Serik tried to run but Noah was stronger than her. She missed a step and fell on the coffee table. Noah picked her up violently and pushed her to the couch. Serik screamed loudly and painfully as Noah hit her.

After the beating, Serik sat in the corner of the living room with torn clothes and messy hair. Blood and purple marks were everywhere on her face, arms, legs and body. Noah whistled in the bathroom like nothing had happened. Luke was hiding in the kitchen after what he saw. Serik secretly changed her clothes in the bedroom and messaged Tam to come to pick her up without saying anything about the attack.

Serik sneaked out of the apartment. She did not close the door properly because she was afraid that Noah would come out to get her if he heard the door. She ran downstairs. Luke came out from the kitchen, saw the open door, and that Serik was not there. He followed Serik's steps to the ground floor. He barked softly just enough for Serik to hear him. When Serik turned around, Luke jumped on Serik and asked her to take him with her.

Tam could not believe her eyes when she saw Serik. She hugged Serik and shed tears. Serik was calm and asked Tam to drive her to the police station to report the attack. Tam called An so that her husband could go straight to the police station to assist.

...

After the sexual abuse, more people knew about Serik as she started a social media campaign to speak up and prevent sexual harassment from husbands or ex-husbands. Their organization got more attention from the public and received some social awards. Serik did not obtain a Dutch passport due to her divorce, but she did not care. Her company sponsored her with a working visa so she could stay in the Netherlands for at least a few years to continue her job. She wrote more articles and stories about domestic violence and about women's role and inequality. She worked hard and more women were rescued and changed their lives completely when they sought out support from VRIENDINEN.

Henk and Max were still Serik's good friends who helped her with the social work. However, Serik knew it was time for her to make decision about which one she would be more serious with. She enjoyed the current situation of dating both of them, but did not go any further. She did not take it as a given that she had to choose one of them to marry so that she could obtain Dutch citizenship.

Max and Serik spent a lot of time hanging out with each other. For example, they travelled together when both of them had a break. They went on holidays and even visited Max's family. They did not admit their relationship or introduced themselves as boyfriend and girlfriend but to many people they were a couple.

Henk knew about Max and that their relationship was closer than his and Serik's. He did not care much as he still hoped that if Serik did not confirm anything it meant that he had chance to win her heart. He asked her out quite often either to visit his winery in France or to spend a weekend at his cottage in Austria. Serik enjoyed the company and she loved the experience he brought but their relationship was just like normal dating, not like with Max.

...

Henk knew that Serik was a big fan of Tiffany & Co. so he bought a jewelry set as a surprise present for Serik. He even prepared a simple but romantic lunch at a famous pancake restaurant in town with some exciting activities after lunch for Serik. He bought a big bouquet of flowers with Serik's favorite color. He took his Jaguar sport's car to the restaurant with a plan to get away with Serik with a trip to Belgium after the lunch. Serik showed up a bit late at the restaurant.

"So sorry, Henk," she said apologetically. "I'm late. I needed to respond to an email from Yale University."

"It's okay, gorgeous. Waiting for you is my pleasure. What are you doing with Yale?" Henk was curious

"Ah, there is good news. I was selected as a candidate for a leadership scholarship at Yale. I've just submitted my portfolio to them. That's why I'm late."

"I see. For a moment, let's forget about Yale, forget about VRIENDI-NEN. Something even more important is coming," Henk tried to drive her attention to what he would say so he ignored her excitement about Yale.

"Oh okay...so?" Serik looked into Henk's eyes

"Serik, I want to learn more about you. I want to spend more time with you not just on vacation or meetings about VRIENDINEN. I want to be your boyfriend," Henk said as he gave Serik the tiffany colored box and the bouquet to show his sincerity. Serik did not know how to respond. She sat back and a thought came to her mind. At that point of time, she knew Henk was not the man she would choose.

"Henk, I can't take it. Can we remain good friends like this? Keep this status," she asked.

Henk's heart was broken, but he respected her choice. Henk smiled and asked Serik if he could give her a hug and a kiss. Serik looked at him lovingly and nodded her head.

...

Serik caught up with Tam at the park where she was playing with her daughter. She sat on the bench watching Tam and her daughter. Her mind was full of thoughts. Tam came up to Serik.

"Hey! I didn't expect you here. You were supposed to be with Henk today, right?"

"Yeah, you're right. I've just left the restaurant."

"How was your lunch? You finished it early aye?" Tam was quite curious.

"Well, he asked me to be his girlfriend but I rejected him," Serik replied while looking around the park.

"Oh really? How come? Have you made up your mind to be with Max?"

"I don't know. Many things are going on now. You know about the leadership scholarship at Yale University that I received recently, don't you?" Serik asked while waving at Tam's daughter and showing her a pack of cookies.

"Hmm, it's time, dear, to make a decision. It's not a game and you can't ride two boats with two legs."

"I know, but Max didn't say anything. We have no plans for this weekend. He's busy, I guess," Serik had no idea why she mentioned Max. It sounded like she was waiting for his action.

...

Max called Serik on Saturday morning to ask her out for dinner. She did not expect this as she thought he was out of town this weekend. However, she could not hide her happiness when Max asked for the date.

Max took her to a fine dining restaurant which she had been wanting to try many times but had no chance. Under the candlelight and a romantic dinner with red wine, Max gave her a flower bouquet. Serik could not hide her surprise, but she guessed what was next. She thought she knew what Max would do.

"Max, what does this mean? Are you...?" She could not finish the sentence. Max already jumped into it and had kneeled down.

"Will you marry me, Serik? My life was so plain until you came in. Please fulfil it with your love," said Max as he took a ring box from his pocket and gave it to Serik.

Serik did not say a word. The silence was softly killing Max. He could feel his heart rapidly beating. He saw the expression on Serik's face and he was nervous. Serik rolled her eyes, touched her nose, looked down at her wine glass, and then she looked into Max's eyes with a smile.

"Max, I think I know the answer. Thanks for loving me, for being with me through hardship and motivating me to get what I have now... but I've made up my mind. I'm sorry, Max. My life has just begun again. I'm gonna take the scholarship to Yale. I've told you about it, right? I'm gonna take it."

Serik smiled joyfully, kissed Max deeply, and left him behind at the restaurant with a goodbye. She took a taxi home and whistled all the way. Serik got home, opened her laptop, and began to write.

...

A few days later, Serik was in a taxi to the airport looking out the window at a sunny day in the Netherlands. She was not sure how long it would be before she would once again see the green grass with so many cows and sheep peacefully grazing. She placed her hand on her chin and leaned on the car door. She smiled happily, then took her phone out of her bag to message her best friend, Tam, "Please check your email. I will see you soon, babe."

Hi Tam!

Sorry to leave without a proper goodbye, but I know I wouldn't be able to hold my tears in and I cannot make this decision. Thanks for being with me through the ups and downs of my life, for being at my back to encourage me. You're my very best friend. I love you.

Max proposed to me, but I said no. I know you might think that I'm so stupid to blow this chance to be the lady of a successful politician with a promising career. I saw the light at the end of the tunnel and now I know what I want for my future. It's not a Dutch passport, not a rich or successful man, and not an award. I want to fulfil myself, to discover my ability, to challenge my boundaries and more than that to help more women stay stronger and fight for their equality.

I've accepted the scholarship from Yale University. When you're reading this email, I will probably be at the airport waiting to board the plane to America. Two years will go by fast, but I have no idea of what's gonna happen after two years. The present is a gift. Our friendship is the best gift I've ever had. This leadership scholarship is an opportunity that I dreamt of and had never touched until now. Dreams comes true, Tam.

I know that my life will be full of adventure and love is just one piece of that journey. My perspective has changed. I can be a global citizen. I will be everywhere, everywhere people need me. Do you still remember what you told me on the day when I was in misery and in the darkest mood of my life? **Ik ben een vechter, een vechter** (I'm a fighter, a fighter). I have to fight for what I want and what I deserve. I will also fight for other women.

I believe that you and An will take good care of VRIENDI-NEN when I'm away. Everywhere I go, I'll try my best to promote our organization and I will carry our vision with me. Never stop fighting for gender equality. Women everywhere deserve to have good lives.

See you soon either in the US or Europe. I'll live well. Don't worry. I'll continue what WE pursue but perhaps in a different context.

Say goodbye to An for me and send my apologies for not giving her a proper goodbye. I'll call you when I arrive.

Take care and I Love You

Xoxo

Serik

Tam closed her laptop and looked out into the garden. Her favorite song was on the radio:

"What doesn't kill you makes you stronger. Stand a little taller. Doesn't mean I'm lonely when I'm alone. What doesn't kill you makes a fire. Put that thing on higher. Doesn't mean I'm over cause you're gone."

Outside the flowers were blooming.

The End

Thu Lan Anh Trang

Thu Lan Anh Trang is a Vietnamese mother of a two-year-old boy living in a small city close to Rotterdam in the Netherlands. When she was still in Ho Chi Minh City, she published an artbook for her father called "Painter – Soldier Trang Phuong" which is about her father's art works together with his story about the American War. She therefore wished that she could have her own book published one day.

She loves writing and has tried to complete a few stories but they remained in her notebook. She had no courage and confidence to publish them. Then she became busy with work and many other distractions which caused her to forget her passion and interest in writing until she joined the **Saigon Writers Club**. These passions came back and now she is confident to share her first story to the public. "Writers write" is one of the mantras of the **Saigon Writers Club** and Thu hopes that this is a good start for her to pursue her dream to become an author and support her travel blog. The name of her travel blog is **Journey of a Frog to the World** and through it she will share her experiences and stories that she has collected on her journey to explore this world.

This story is based on a real person who is a friend of mine living in the same city in the Netherlands. Of course, the person is true, but the character and story were built up. What she experienced motivated me to write something about it and build a dream character that I wished she could become. We knew each other from a workshop organized by the city council when Covid-19 was less tense. As new immigrants with Asian backgrounds to a Western country, we easily understood each other and became good friends. The ending in the story is what I wished for her, but the reality was unknown. When I completed my short story and came back to the Netherlands after my holiday in Vietnam, I could not contact her anymore. She disappeared on WhatsApp and her phone number was inactive. I have tried many ways but so far have been unsuccessful to get in touch with her again. She gave up this friendship without a word... However, I do hope I can reach her at some point of my life here or there and it will be like what the character said at the end of the story to her friend.